10

WHAT'S DONE IS DONE

CORINNA TURNER

PRAISE FOR CORINNA TURNER'S BOOKS

LIBERATION: nominated for the *Carnegie Medal Award 2016*
ELFLING: 1st prize, Teen Fiction, *CPA Book Awards 2019*
I AM MARGARET & *BANE'S EYES:* finalists, *CALA Award 2016/2018*
LIBERATION & *THE SIEGE OF REGINALD HILL:* 3rd place, *CPA Book
Awards 2016/2019*

Corinna Turner was awarded the **St. Katherine Drexel Award** in
2022.

PRAISE FOR *ELFLING*

I was instantly drawn in

EOIN COLFER, author of *Artemis Fowl* and former Children's Laureate
of Ireland

PRAISE FOR *WHAT'S DONE IS DONE*

*Corinna Turner has done it again with this exciting and
suspenseful addition to her unSPARKed series. This latest
installment is sure to please the dinosaur-lover in all her
readers!*

ANTONY BARONE KOLENC, author of the award-winning
medieval series, The Harwood Mysteries

PRAISE FOR THE UNSPARKED SERIES

*Beware: this series' vivid descriptions, heart-pounding drama,
and fabulous characters are sure to lure you in, as well.*

LESLEA WAHL, author of the Blindside series

A cross between Jurassic World *and* Mad Max! *Fun, fast paced.
And sets up an incredible new world. I read it three times in two
days!*

STEVEN R. MCEVOY, BookReviewsAndMore Blogger

ALSO BY CORINNA TURNER:

I AM MARGARET series
For older teens and up

Brothers (*A Prequel Novella*)*
1: I Am Margaret*
1: Io Sono Margaret (Italian)
2: The Three Most Wanted*
3: Liberation*
4: Bane's Eyes*
5: Margo's Diary*
6: The Siege of Reginald Hill*
7: A Saint in the Family*
'The Underappreciated Virtues of Rusty Old Bicycles' (*Prequel short story*) Also found in the anthology: Secrets: Visible & Invisible*

I Am Margaret: The Play (*Adapted by Fiorella de Maria*)

UNSPARKED series
For tweens and up

Main Series:
1: Please Don't Feed the Dinosaurs*
2: A Truly Raptor-ous Welcome*
3: PANIC!*
4: Farmgirls Die in Cages*
5: Wild Life*
6: A Right Rex Rodeo
7: FEAR
8: A Different Kind of Camouflage
9: A Different Kind of Freedom
10: What's Done is Done
11: Weigh the Odds†

Prequels:
BREACH!*
A Mom With Blue Feathers†
A Very Jurassic Christmas*

Short Stories (ebook only):
'Liam and the Hunters of Lee'Vi'
'A Truly Clawful Christmas'*
'A Very Jurassic Lent'
Also available as a paperback:
Three Clawsome Tales

FRIENDS IN HIGH PLACES series
For tweens and up

1: The Boy Who Knew (Carlo Acutis)*
2: Old Men Don't Walk to Egypt (Saint Joseph)*
3: Child, Unwanted (Margaret of Castello)*
4: A Lion for a Tomb (Ignatius of Antioch)

Do Carpenter's Dream of Wooden Sheep? (*Spin-off, comes between 1 & 2*)

1: El Chico Que Lo Sabia (Spanish)
1: Il Ragazzo Che Sapeva (Italian)

YESTERDAY & TOMORROW series
For adults and mature teens only
Someday: A Novella*
Eines Tages (German)
1: Tomorrow's Dead†

OTHER WORKS

For teens and up
Elfling*
'The Most Expensive Alley Cat in London' (Elfling *prequel short story*)

For tweens and up
Mandy Lamb & The Full Moon*
The Wolf, The Lamb, and The Air Balloon (Mandy Lamb *novella*)

For adults and new adults
Three Last Things *or* The Hounding of Carl Jarrold, Soulless Assassin*
A Changing of the Guard*
The Raven & The Yew†

† Coming Soon
*** Awarded the Catholic Writers Guild**
Seal of Approval

CONTENTS

JOSHUA

"Wilson?" The mail guy peers in through the hatch.

Something for me? I jump down from my bunk and hurry the few steps to the cell door.

"Thanks." It's an official-looking envelope. Is it something to do with my release in a week's time?

Have they changed their minds?

Such a jolt of terror goes through me that I can't even wait to get back to my bunk. I rip it right open; yank out the sheets of paper inside.

My heart's pounding so hard and the rush of adrenalin is so strong, I have to re-read the first sentence a couple of times to take it in. Nothing to do with my release, *thank God, thank Saint Des*. It's about Wilhelm...about his will...

I move back to my bunk and climb up without looking, my eyes on the letter.

"No bad news, then?" asks Ku, watching me, eyes intent in his slightly lined face. He's sitting at the desk under what used to be Billy's bunk when Billy lived here in 'Hunter One,' instead of in 'Hunter Two,' the neighboring cell.

"No, it's all okay." I don't say no more, trying to take in what the letter's saying. *...wish to inform you that Wilhelm Fenn made you a behest in his will, consisting of a twenty-five percent share in the Habitation Vehicle registration number HUH6 JFK4. Mr. Fenn placed a restriction on the behest to the effect that possession of said share cannot be taken up by yourself in any way until after the death of one Sebastian Stevens, your co-owner of Habitation Vehicle registration number HUH6 JFK4.*

Leaving someone your share in a Hab'Vi—normal. The second provision—not. I guess the lawyers and everyone will assume it's to protect Seb's livelihood, but I ain't under no such illusions. It's to protect *me* from Seb. If someone he can't control ends up with that share, Seb might just arrange an accident for them. After all, this is the guy who took money to kill Darryl and Harry's father. And if he didn't end up doing it with his own hands in the end, it's only because he realized he could make more money by selling William Franklyn to someone with a personal interest in doing the bloody deed himself.

And Seb dragged Wilhelm into it, and Wilhelm were too weak and scared to say no...

I sigh, fold the letter and return it to the envelope, then stare up at the ceiling. One more week, and I'm outta here. I should be ecstatic, but Wilhelm's death almost a month ago casts a shadow over everything, even that.

I tilt the envelope and stare at the address, the address that soon won't be mine no more.

#75649271
(Joshua Wilson)
Exception Central Penitentiary
Exception City
Exception State

You didn't have to do this, Wilhelm. But I guess he didn't have no one else. I guess I really was the person he wanted to give his most prized possession to. We shared a cell for three and a half months, we were friends. Even finding out what he did to Darryl and Harry's dad can't change that. I miss him.

...possession of said share cannot be taken up by yourself in any way until after the death of one Sebastian Stevens...

Why did you always call yourself thick, Wilhelm? That just proves you ain't.

Or that he knew Seb *far* too well after being stuck with him for eight years in a partnership from hell.

+

Click. Clank.

I glance up in surprise as the cell door slides open, leaving us free to roam the wing. Pre-lunch tier-time already?

Billy stumps in only moments later and Ku moves to his bunk so Billy can take the desk chair and whittle with his illicit carving tools, the way he always did when he were still living in this cell. Through the doorway, Caleb's legs peep into view as he settles on the floor, ostensibly chilling out on the balcony outside Hunter One, but in reality avoiding being alone next door in Hunter Two.

His older brother Jason certainly proved at my expense—and Wilhelm's—the inadvisability of letting some unfriendly person trap you inside a cell. The inter-cell concrete walls are surprisingly thick—you don't hear as much of what's going on next door as you might expect. So, once Billy comes in here to hang out with us, Caleb lurks just outside to benefit from that mutual Hunter protection I insisted he still has a right to, whether we three like him or not. Too many of the city thugs in here think picking on the one-armed guy is great fun.

Ku and Billy begin the kinda familiar chit-chat-bicker-banter you expect from guys who've co-owned a 'Vi since forever. Billy's only in Hunter Two with Caleb because it ain't safe for me to share with Caleb when he stood guard while his brother tried to kill me.

If only Ku and Billy had been prepared to protect Wilhelm the way they protect me.

Ambushed by an increasingly familiar wave of anger, I fold the envelope and shove it in my pocket, then jump down from my bunk and head out onto the balcony, leaning on the rail. Ironically, since Caleb had far more to do with Wilhelm's death than Billy or Ku, I often find it easier to come out here for a while. I guess Caleb don't try to make conversation with me.

Not normally, anyway. He's just risen to his feet and come to stand beside me, the stump of his left arm resting on the rail—everything missing from just below his elbow joint. He has a mounting he can strap on and use with a set of handy attachments, apparently, but the city-folk confiscated all of them— too sharp or pointy—except the 'vanity hand' as Jason would sneer, and Caleb don't care to wear that.

"Morning, Caleb," I say, 'cause I've been trying real hard to be civil to the guy. He ain't a shining example of humanity, but in the last year he lost his hand, his (okay, cruel and illegal) business, his freedom, and his brother—Jason ain't been sentenced yet for what he did to Wilhelm and me, but he's gonna get such a long sentence he won't be coming back to this medium-sentence wing. It ain't clear if Caleb misses Jason for his own sake, but he sure misses having him at his back, and with reason.

"Morning, cub."

I'm too used to guys Caleb's age calling me cub to protest. At least he left off "mewling." Mebbe he's reforming.

After a moment, he speaks again—flatly. "You never asked me how I lost my hand."

Uh-oh.

"Do I need to?"

"You might be interested. After you let them fifty juvenile rex out into the feed alley we were all standing in..." He breaks off, shaking his head. "You're mad, cub!"

"After you honest-to-God *ran* down that alley, under the noses of fifty juvenile rex? Seriously, Caleb? Call yourself hunter-born!"

He scowls. "It weren't as dumb as you make it sound," he snaps. "If I'd come for them electric prods behind you, you and the farm-kids would've jumped me."

"You should've just stood still. Or walked *slowly*."

"Sure, while you and the kids edged away and escaped! Jason woulda ripped my guts out!"

"You're his brother."

"Yeah? I've tried that one. Those rex knew people always came with electric prods. I thought they'd hold off just long enough for me to get a prod. Then I coulda chased 'em back into their pens real quick and re-captured you three. Jason wouldn't have been mad at me, then. But that darn cocky one year-old—never did like that one. The motion were too much for it and it lunged at me."

"Yeah, s'why you *don't run*," I mutter, though pity stabs me at the thought that this guy were so scared of his own *brother* that he did something so reckless.

Caleb shoots me another glare. "Anyway, it ripped up my lower arm, coupla long, deep gashes, but I put a few bullets into its head—not rex caliber but enough to sting. Drove it off long enough for me to get into the gap between one of the open sliding gates and the pen wall and shimmy up high enough to reach the part where the bars are narrower than their muzzles. I were safe in there until Jason finally turned up and re-penned the few remaining rex."

Caleb shudders. "Heck, he were mad. Yelled at me, swore bloody death on you. But they dragged me back into the bunkhouse and Jason left Gerry to clean and staple my wounds while he took Nashoba and went straight out after the rex. He knew he were gonna have to shoot most of 'em, only way to contain the situation. He were *furious*."

"Yeah? And I thought he tried to drown me in your toilet because he were only mildly peeved."

"Very funny, Wilson. Anyway, I knew the arm were bad—I couldn't move my fingers hardly at all. Nerves were damaged. Kinda thing a city-hospital can usually fix, and when he finally came back for a break

I begged him to take me there, but he refused. He said he'd take me when all the rex were dealt with and my arm would be fine until then."

"Nerve-damage? Every hour counts."

"Heck, I knew that. But Jason had the 'Vi, and he just kept shooting me up with more morphine to quiet me down. I still don't know if Jace meant it, but were deluding himself how long it were gonna take him, or if he had no intention of ever letting me go nowhere near a hospital in case something came out about the rex farm. Anyway, three days later, he'd barely shot twenty of the darn rex and my arm were rotting. Gangrene."

I wince. "So he took you to the hospital then?"

Caleb snorts. "Too late for that. He chopped my arm off and cauterized it with a hot iron. Saved my life, sure, but it wouldn't have been necessary if he'd just taken me to the *misfiring* hospital in the first place." The cold rage in Caleb's voice echoes the coldness in my belly at what he's telling me. "I coulda kept the hand. I coulda got most of the use back, probably. Except for that greedy..." He goes off into a real imaginative description of his older brother that involves a lotta words Saint Des don't appreciate.

So, one of their unlicensed rex *didn't* bite his hand off. It were Jason? I am interested to hear that. Honestly, it makes me feel better about my part in it all.

"So, sure, Wilson, I blame you for losing this hand," growls Caleb at last. "But it's a fifty-fifty split with my dear brother."

"Sounds more like seventy-five to Jason and twenty to you for running and only five to me," I can't help saying.

Caleb just glowers.

"Are you sure that's how it happened?" I try to speak lightly. "I heard a guy telling some fresh fish about it the other day. Apparently us other hunters cut it off and ate it in some secret cook-out with lighters 'cause we don't like you or some'at."

He snorts. "No, that were a *mouse*. I've heard all about *that*."

"Oh yeah, so it were."

He stares down into the hall, his amusement draining away quicker than it came, then jerks his head over his shoulder toward Hunter One. "Them two's gonna kick me outta the pack again the moment you're gone. Y'know that, right?"

"No, they ain't. Why d'you think that?"

He snorts again. "They only took me back in 'cause the poor bereaved cub stomped his little paws and insisted. You ain't gonna be here to appeal to their better natures for much longer."

"They ain't gonna kick you out!"

An even bleaker snort. I shoot him a look. His expression is trying for grim, but I can see the fear underneath. He really thinks they're gonna throw him to the wolves, don't he? And then his life would be a living hell.

"Anyway..." His hand slips inside his lurid orange jacket, and I tense, but it comes out holding...my heart clenches. "They, uh, packed up Fenn's stuff, but, uh, Jace had took this. Guess you've more right to it than he does."

I reach out a hand and accept the angel singer, a circle of crisscrossing cords edged with colorful raptor ruff feathers, with three silent chimes hanging below. Woven into the circle are a mouse skeleton and the trail sign for 'friend.'

"This is how Jason knew to use Wilhelm as bait," I say flatly.

Another snort from Caleb, derisive this time. "*That weren't hard to figure out, cub.*"

I guess it don't really matter where or when the confrontation with Jason had taken place, Wilhelm might have defended me just the same, and with the same result. *What ifs never helped anyone*, Dad used to say. It ain't my fault Wilhelm's dead.

It's Jason's.

+

Three days. I stare at the fence around the exercise yard; at the wall beyond. Three days, and I'll be on the other side of that. It feels kinda surreal, hard to picture, after nine months locked up.

Nearby, Caleb also stares glumly at the fence. Every day that passes he grows grimmer-faced and more jumpy. I'd like to think he's worrying for nothing, but I've caught Billy giving him a mean look or two. Billy was far more annoyed than Ku about taking Caleb back in. Guess now Wilhelm's dead he feels bad for always being nasty to him, but Jason's gone so the only person to be mad at—other than himself—is Caleb.

A burst of shouting from across the yard makes Caleb turn. I glance around as well. Two rival gangs of city-guys are getting real heated with one another. My heart sinks. Our yard time's barely started, but if it kicks off, the guards will fire into the ground and we'll have three seconds to get flat or they'll shoot us—and then we'll all have to go straight back inside.

Oh, who cares? In three days I can have all the time I like outside in the open air. As soon as I find an assistant, anyway. I won't be able to take Darryl and Harry out-city with me. I can't even *see* them without messing up Darryl's plans to get custody of Harry. They may be the only family I have now, but the city-folk say they ain't my blood relatives so I'd no right to take them nowhere—even though they wanted to go.

And, honestly, however desperate I am to see them, I ain't risking getting slung straight back into prison. We're gonna have to wait. Unless they wanna lit out to another state. I'd be up for that, I guess. But I doubt they do. They have their farm to think about.

Of course, this is all assuming their dad *is* dead. I might know more about that when I see Father Ben in three days. But it's been the better part of two years with no word, and from what Wilhelm told me… Yeah, he's dead, all right. But we gotta check out everything we can, and find out for definite how it happened and who did it. For Darryl and Harry's sake. Whether we can actually get justice…well. We'll have to see about that. I don't see how we can touch Seb or the money guy, with only my word about what Wilhelm told me. As for the guy who actually killed William Franklyn…? Proving it will be the thing.

Caleb's now staring at the city-guys like he ain't even seeing them, his shoulders slumped. I'm getting kinda worried about him. I guess I should talk to Ku and Billy…

The shouting swells as the two groups surge together, interspersed with meaty sounds of fists striking flesh.

Here we go…

Yep. Sharp reports echo from the towers.

"Shots fired, down on the ground!" shout the perimeter guards. "Down, now!"

I've started to dip toward the scraggly grass when I realize Caleb ain't moved. He's just standing, with a fixed look on his face. He's twenty-foot away and I ain't got enough seconds left, but…

I sprint.

Three point five seconds later I slam into Caleb and carry him to the ground. We hit hard, but I put all my weight on him.

"Stay…*down*," I gasp, in between winded breaths. "I don't…wanna…get shot…today!"

But he don't struggle. Just lies there.

Yeah, he's getting himself in a bad way, ain't he?

Why do I even care?

'Cause I've walked that road, I guess, and it stinks.

We lie motionless until a pair of uniform boots appear beside us.

"Wilson, Desmoines, what's going on? Are you fighting?"

I glance up to see Hurst, one of the oldest and most genial guards, looking down at us.

I leave go of Caleb at last and sit up. "No, Caleb was just in a real world of his own. So I pulled him down so he wouldn't get shot."

No need to embarrass Caleb by getting real specific. Hurst can figure it out.

"Desmoines," says Hurst at once. "Get up. Chaplain or sick bay, take your pick."

Yep.

Scowling, Caleb rises to his feet. After a moment, he mutters, "Chaplain."

A couple of guards lead him away while the rest of us are ushered back into line.

Soon—with a *clunk, click* as the door locks behind us—Ku and I are back in Hunter One.

"Ku, you and Billy *need* to talk to Caleb," I say immediately.

"Guess he's losing it, but what can *we* do?"

"He thinks you're gonna kick him outta the pack as soon as I'm gone, *that's* what's tipped him over the edge. Are you?"

Ku snorts. "You kidding? A pack of three—or two and a half, as Billy would say—is small enough."

"Then make that clear to him. Or you'll be a pack of two."

+

My eyes are gritty and heavy as I hug Ku goodbye—I didn't sleep one wink last night. I clasp shoulders more awkwardly with Billy. Caleb's just placed his box of belongings on my—no, his!—top bunk, so I reach for his shoulder too. His jaw slackens slightly in surprise, then he hesitantly returns the grip.

After Caleb got back from the Chaplain the other day, Ku called to him to stop lurking outside and sit himself down in the cell, so since then he's been hanging out inside Hunter One instead. Ku and Billy don't talk to him much, but Ku handed him the box of candied apples his daughter sent him when passing it around to the rest of us, and it all seems to have convinced him that they do consider him permanent pack. At any rate, he's gone back to being merely morose. Guess he ain't got much to be cheerful about, only a few months into his ten-year sentence.

"Bye, cub," says Ku, as I pick up my box of belongings and move to the door, my heart pounding far harder than the amount of exercise requires. "Stay outta trouble."

"Bye, Raptor Boy," says Billy. "No more rex riding."

"Bye, Wilson," mutters Caleb.

"Bye, prison pack. Look me up when you get out."

I step through the door and follow the guard along the tier and down the stairs. When we reach the double-layer door outta the wing I glance up. All three hunters are standing by the rail. They raise their hands in farewell. I give an awkward hand-flap back, restricted by my box. And then I'm through the first door. And then the second.

We don't head down the passages toward the entrance, though. My steps begin to drag as I glance around warily.

"Warden wants to see you before you go," explains the guard, stopping outside an unusually fancy door, made of wood instead of metal, although the window beside it is standard reinforced prison safety glass. He points to a table. "You can put your box there."

Is this normal? Does everyone see the warden on their way out? I reckon not. But, obediently, I place the box down and follow the guard to the door. The guard opens it and gestures me past him, leaning in to say, "Joshua Wilson, sir."

"Thank you." The warden—a tall, thin man who always reminds me of a gray heron—waves a dismissal, and the guard withdraws. "So, Mr. Wilson—oh, you can sit down—you're out today. Excited?"

Cautiously, I settle in the chair opposite the desk and answer the dumb question in the only possible way. "Uh, yeah?"

"Yes, of course you are. Well, personally, I'm sorry to see you go. The literacy rates in B wing have never been better. I see we need to replace our handwriting classes with cursive classes."

"That won't work." I speak without thinking. Uh-oh, did I come across as mouthy?

"Oh?" He merely raises a thin eyebrow.

"Uh, I mean, if you just *replace* 'em, you might as well *call* 'em handwriting classes. But if you added cursive classes *as well*… That might help."

"Ah. Yes. Indeed. I will think about that. Well, that wasn't actually why I needed to see you, though I'm glad of an opportunity to thank you for your good work. It's actually about Wilhelm Fenn."

My stomach lurches, the way it still does every time Wilhelm is mentioned. I don't say nothing.

"I believe you were friends, so first of all, I'm sorry for your loss."

"Thank you," I mutter.

"Secondly," he reaches behind the desk, then straightens, placing an ugly gallon-sized plastic jar on the desktop. "We have been trying to track down family or friends to take charge of Mr. Fenn's remains, but without success."

Still? Have they got him frozen in a freezer or something? "Well," I say reluctantly, "Seb's his co-owner."

The warden wrinkles up his nose as though something unpleasant is under it. "Mr. Stevens has declined to take on the responsibility. Your friendship with Mr. Fenn was brought to my attention, so it seems appropriate to offer you the opportunity, otherwise Mr. Fenn's remains must be interred in the prison plot."

What? No way; I'm not leaving Wilhelm in here, forever! "I'll deal with it. How do I…uh…where do I collect him from?"

Surprise widens the warden's eyes. He shifts the plastic jar a fraction. "Right here?"

I stare at the jar. Only now do I notice that it has a name typed on it: Wilhelm Fenn. And his prison number. "What…? He wouldn't fit in—" Then it clicks. City-folk burn their dead to cinders. Horror and outrage bubbling up like lava, I surge from my seat, my hands slamming down on the desk. "What did you *do*? You…you barbarians, you *pagan*—"

As the door flies open and the guard dashes in, I drop back into my seat like I've been shot, hunching to make myself look as harmless as possible. "I'm sorry! I'm sorry, I weren't gonna do nothing! Don't make me stay!" Terror sends a second—freezing—wave of adrenaline through me.

Eyeing me closely, the warden waves the guard back out. "You're upset." That's a statement, not a question. "Why? The cremation was carried out in a completely normal manner. No disrespect intended."

"But he was a *hunter*! He shoulda been buried!" Despite my fear that I've overstepped, the words come out heated. "We don't do that thing…burning people. We don't *do that*!"

Actually…now the first flush of shock is passing off…Wilhelm were city-born. So mebbe I care more than he does. But it's still *horrible*. And he were a hunter, all his adult working life. He shoulda been buried decently.

I'm actually shaking slightly as my shock and the fear that hit me when the guard entered combine against me. I swallow and draw a few deep breaths. "I'll take charge of him," I say, finally. But can't stop myself adding, "*What's left of him.*"

The warden tents his fingers, watching me over them. "So it's culturally unacceptable for hunters to be cremated?"

"Ones that follow Saint Des, yeah. And that's most

of us. It's a Catholic thing, though I think city Catholics ain't so strict about it."

"I see. Then I offer my apologies to you and to the hunter community. As you know, the numbers of hunters in prison is very low—we will skip the debate as to whether hunters are more law abiding or merely a hundred times harder to catch. Be that as it may, Mr. Fenn was the first hunter to pass away in this prison who did not have relatives waiting to arrange every-thing, and so I was not aware of the difference in funeral practice. What's done is done. But I assure you such an error will not occur again under my watch."

"Uh...thank you, sir."

"Very well, I'm sure you've no wish to sit here with me when you could be outside celebrating. Off with you, then, young man."

"Er...yes, sir. Thank you, sir."

I grab the ugly plastic jar from the desk—the least I can do is give what's left a proper burial—and hurry from the room. The guard eyes what I'm holding and, unlike me, clearly recognizes it immediately.

"I'll, uh...I'll get this for you." Double-quick, he picks up my box, like he's afraid he might have to carry the ashes.

Like I'd hand them to him. I hug the jar tightly to my chest and hurry after the guard, my throat tight, but my eyes dry. I'm still in prison, so I ain't safe. I ain't cried for what, nine months? Do I still know how?

In 'Processing' I change my lurid orange outfit for my own camo trousers and checkered shirt plus a warm camo jacket and boots Fr. Ben dropped around ready, since I were captured barefoot from my sick bed. I finger the green and brown splotched cotton, the familiarity/unfamiliarity jarring me like the recoil from a real heavy rex gun.

And then the guard's escorting me to the main door. And I'm stepping through—with no shackles this time!

"Is, uh, someone picking you up?" the guard asks, still lugging my box and eyeing the jar of ashes warily, like being cremated might be contagious.

"Yeah. Oh, over there." I nod to where a black van with a white dorsal stripe is parked in the prison parking lot. A broad-shouldered priest in sturdy black outdoor wear, a clerical collar, and a black Stetson already strides toward us, a broad smile making his teeth gleam against his dark skinned face.

"Father Ben! They really let me out!" I hurry toward him, almost regretting saying the words before I'm in his van and driving through the gates.

"Of course they did!" he grins. Then his eyes fall on what I'm clutching. "Oh dear. Is that…? Are you all right, Josh? You look a bit…" He trails off, his eyes narrowed in concern.

"Yeah, it's Wilhelm, all right. What's left! The city-folk burned him up and stuck him in this jar; can you believe it? And that snake Seb wouldn't do what was right and decent by him. So they gave him to me."

"Ah. Oh, thank you, I can take that." Father Ben relieves the guard of my box of belongings. "You bring the urn, Josh. At least he's in good hands now. Come on, let's get out of here. Strange thing"—he winks at me—"I don't enjoy prison visiting quite as much as I used to."

+

I expect to relax once we're through the gates and driving down the road, but I'm shaking more and more, the 'urn' cradled in my lap. I feel chilled and clammy. Ain't I meant to be happy? But this Wilhelm thing's knocked me for a loop. Yet again. I wanna hibernate or some'at until my head stops spinning and my guts stop churning.

"Josh? We'll have a real nice burial for Wilhelm, okay? And remember, it may not be the preferred way to do things, but God's more than capable of dealing with it, right?"

"Yeah, I know that," I mutter.

"Good. Look, if you're feeling like up is down, that's a very common reaction to a huge life change like being released from prison. Being handed that urn all unexpectedly will only have made it worse. So just try to relax and ride the mood out. Make sense?"

I thought I'd just be happy today. So happy. But Father Ben knows what he's talking about. He's even been through it himself, though they only put him away for three months for helping us. If he says I'm gonna feel all discombobulated, I believe him. Hard not to, since I do!

I expect him to turn onto the main city ring road, but he takes a left instead, pulling into a tiny patch of artificially landscaped greenery past a sign that reads: Exception City Park & Reserve. "Ain't we going to the 'Vi-park? You said my HabVi were fine."

"Your Habitat Vehicle *is* fine. You, however, need a hot coffee."

"I can have one as soon as I'm home in the 'Vi!"

Father Ben's only response is to pull into a space in the mostly empty parking lot and switch off the engine. "Let's just grab a coffee from the visitor center and sit under the trees for a few minutes until you feel better, okay?"

Not okay. But he's made time in his busy schedule to come and pick me up, so I manage to bite my tongue. I open the door and get out, trying not to scuff my feet like a sulky kid. I keep hold of the urn, though.

Fr. Ben's eyes fix on it as he comes around the van. "Why don't you leave that in there?"

"What if some city-thief breaks in and takes it?"

"Hardly likely." I must look mulish, because he adds, "Well, bring it, then." A thoughtful look enters his eyes. "Yes, why don't you get a nice gift bag from the shop to put it in? Much more respectful than that truly awful excuse for an urn."

"I can make something better as soon as I get home. Assuming the authorities didn't make off with all my handicrafting supplies." I should have a fine stock of claws and teeth and feathers from all kinds of 'saurs back at the 'Vi. Leathers, too.

"You can, but let's get something right away. It will make you feel better."

Will it? But I follow as he leads the way to the visitor center at the end of the huge parking lot, quiet on this early December morning. It's full of stuffed toys and gift items for tourists to buy, though why anyone would feel the need to commemorate coming to a tiny little patch of greenery like this is beyond me.

Dutifully, I examine the gift bags. Some are quite fancy, with flocked patterns or shimmery effects. One with black flowers is suitably somber, another has plants on, which evokes Soil and Leaf, so might be better. In the end, though, I select a child's one covered in colorful, cheerful little 'saurs.

"Wilhelm would like this best," I explain to Father Ben as I slide the urn into it, pretending not to notice the sidelong look from the cashier.

"Then it's the right one for the job," Father Ben says. "Now, why don't you go and enjoy those trees over there while I grab us a couple of coffees? Bet you haven't seen a tree for a while, huh?"

"I sure ain't." He don't need to suggest *this* twice.

I head that way and run my hand around the trunks. Beech, ash, oak. Healthy enough, despite the city fumes, their winter-bare branches towering overhead. This one's climbable, even with a bagged urn hanging from my arm. I lie on my back on a fat horizontal branch, letting my legs swing and staring up at the sky. No city in sight. Wonderful.

I plunk the urn on my stomach for safety. Father Ben were right. I do feel better now it's respectfully clad in that bag. As the branches wave gently above, I can almost feel the stress draining outta me.

"Hey." A bossy voice. "You can't be up there."

I turn my head to look. A middle-aged guy in some kinda uniform is staring up at me.

"Why not?"

"You might fall and hurt yourself."

"I might *what*?"

"Hurt yourself."

I stare at him. "You think this is dangerous? Try raptor hunting."

He sniffs. "No one in their right mind would go raptor hunting."

"No?" I sit up so he can see my clothes better.

"*Hunters*." He takes the Lord's name in vain, so I cross myself pointedly, though I think it's lost on him. "You're all insane. Look, fine, this may be the safest thing you'll do this year, but you still have to get down. It's a matter of insurance."

"Insurance?" City-folk. Deranged. Totally deranged. But I don't plan on getting slung straight back in prison for climbing a darn tree, so with a big sigh and eye roll, I lower myself by one arm, Wilhelm's bag safely held in the other hand, and drop lightly to the ground just as Father Ben approaches holding two coffee cups.

"Is everything okay?" he asks.

"It is now," says the park guard, or whatever he is, eyeing me warily and then making a hasty escape.

"City-folk ain't allowed to climb trees, even?"

Father Ben shrugs. "City-owned ones, I guess not. Or maybe he's bored. Well, it's easier to drink coffee sitting on a warm, dry bench, anyway."

The coffee's cooling fast in the cold air. My first sip warms me from the inside out, and I realize Father Ben's right again. I do need this. He's put sugar in it, but I don't say nothing.

He's probably right about that, too.

"So, did you find anything out?" I ask.

"I'll tell you back at the 'Vi," he replies.

+

Father Ben don't force us to linger over our coffee, and soon enough we're pulling into the 'Vi-park. It's empty, except for my own happy home parked in the far corner. As we approach, I feast my eyes on the huge, blocky, gray vehicle with its domed observation turret sticking up from the roof. I specifically asked

Father Ben to tell my friends in Technicolor 'Vi to stay away today. I don't quite trust that awful Fernanda Matthews from the CPS not to be lurking, waiting to see which HabVi is here to welcome me. It probably ain't too late for her to go after my "accomplices."

But there's no one here at all. Despite my sensible precaution, I can't help feeling slightly bereft. Silly. I can visit Technicolor at their new camp soon enough.

Someone's already taken the tarpaulins off the Wilson 'Vi, though. I bet they've reconnected the battery and filled the oil and everything ready, too. My heart lifts a little.

As soon as Father Ben pulls up beside the 'Vi I'm reaching for Wilhelm's bag, keen to get out. But Father Ben takes it from me and pops it through into the back, where my box sits. "We can come out for your things in a moment."

"But I wanted to take that in right away…"

"Just trust me on this, Josh. Let's go straight in."

Bewildered, I open the door and get out. I'm considering opening the sliding side door to retrieve the urn regardless, when a thought pops into my head that might explain Father Ben's odd behavior. A thought I can't allow myself to consider for one second, in case it ain't true. But I head straight to the 'Vi, all the same.

The familiar/unfamiliar hiss as the door slides open actually brings a lump to my throat. I vault up into the living area. As Father Ben climbs up behind me, using the foothold, I peer around. The lights are on but the shutters closed and my eyes need to adjust slightly to the dimmer illumination.

Someone's just stood up from a chair by the fold-out table. A bit shorter than me, a feminine — completely, wonderfully feminine — figure. Light skin, brown hair, drawn back — in a braid, no doubt. Even her face has matured, every line womanly, now.

Darryl.

DARRYL

I look up as the door hisses open, my heart suddenly pounding in my chest like a pile driver. A figure leaps up into the 'Vi, silhouetted against the bright sunlight. But it can't be Josh — the shoulders are far too broad, everything too…too *man*-shaped.

But it is. One glimpse of his face as he moves further in, and I stumble to my feet. His black hair is so short, buzzed to mere stubble, and there's a new hardness, a guardedness about him, but it's Josh.

His gaze fixes on me, and he goes motionless. Does he blame me? For what happened to him? Nine *months* in prison…

But his eyes…his brown eyes devour me, much as mine devour him, ticking off familiar things, noting the unfamiliar…

"Josh?" My voice comes out strangled.

"Darryl…"

He takes three steps, I take three steps, then his arms are tight around me, and I wrap mine around him as though I'll never let go again. He buries his face in my hair, and I wish I could do the same, but his prison fuzz merely tickles my nose, failing to absorb the tears running from my eyes.

I inhale, though, and through a host of unfamiliar, unfriendly scents, I catch a trace that's just Josh. Pure Josh. For the first time in almost a year, I feel…safe. Whole.

I hold him and hold him and hold him, and he holds me, and I don't ever wanna let him go, not ever, ever, ever… I can't, I won't, I—

Father Ben's standing right there. I guess Josh remembers at the same moment, 'cause suddenly we're both letting go of each other, stepping apart.

"There was absolutely no hugging before," I say quickly, my cheeks heating up with the speed and intensity of Uncle Mau's state of the art retro-style grill.

"No hugging. Whatsoever," says Josh, sounding inarticulate. "At all."

Father Ben just smiles. "I know," is all he says.

"Oh," says Josh.

"Good," I say. I glance at Josh again. I can't believe how…how grown-up he looks. I mean, I always saw him as the grown-up, but now…he's really filled out, grown into himself. I guess he is twenty now, just like I'm eighteen. Do I look different to him, too? Does he like what he sees? He doesn't seem able to take his eyes off me, any more than I can take mine from him.

I can't believe we're finally together again, yet I can, because it feels so totally right.

But it won't be for long, not unless…

"Father Ben? West said you'd found out something about Dad?"

"Josh did. In prison. And I've done some research. But we'd better wait for Harry, say everything once only."

Josh's eyes light up. "Harry's coming too?"

"Yeah," I say. "Should get here any time."

"But what about your parole?" Josh asks. "I mean, custody. Oh, you know."

I pick up a shaggy black wig and a pair of full-wrap hunter-style sunglasses from the table. "I went into the ladies room and put a complete disguise on, changed my clothes, came out looking nothing like myself—my city self," I add, because he's eyeing my perfectly normal hunter attire with a puzzled air. "I'll do it in reverse when I leave. Harry's doing the same. Fernanda won't know. Anyway, this is *Dad*. We have to risk it."

"Yeah, I guess so. If it all comes to nothing we could just lit out for another state, anyway."

"I've gone suddenly and inexplicably deaf," says

Father Ben, sticking a finger in his ear and wiggling it around. "Strictly temporary, I'm sure."

Okay, he doesn't want us to talk about anything that illegal in front of him. Fair enough. He's already done time for helping us, and he's taking a risk for us all over again. I mean, he's not strictly supposed to be near Harry, and Josh definitely isn't. They could get him again just for this.

I wanna know about Dad, but it's no hardship to just enjoy being with Josh. His hand reaches out tentatively; I slip mine into it. There are so many things I want to say and I can't think of anything to say. We stand in silence, fingers gripping tightly, until the door hisses back again and a stocky, busty hunter girl wearing a heavily decorated leather dress climbs clumsily up into the 'Vi.

Josh snorts out loud—then looks surprised, like he hasn't laughed for a while.

"Am I good, or am I good?" says Harry, putting a hand on his hip in an exaggeratedly feminine pose, though his cheeks are getting redder by the moment. "I shoulda been a spy, right?"

The moment is rather spoiled when Perky the rodentosaur suddenly sticks his head out of the neck of the dress, then scrambles all the way out and up onto Harry's shoulder, leaving Harry completely flat-chested.

Father Ben is laughing hysterically now, and so am

I.

When Josh raises his wrist, pointing his ScreamerBand Harry's way, Harry lunges, pulling his arm down—"No, no photos!"—then getting drawn in for a big hug.

As soon as the hug is over—"Ugh, I'm taking it off. I can't stand it"—Harry abandons his attempt at cool, pulling the dress off over his head—dislodging a blond wig in the process and revealing his own short brown hair—then lobbing the dress into the corner, only to immediately hurry to retrieve it. "Ag, I promised Trudy I'd take care of it…" He drapes it more carefully over a chair, grabbing Perky when he sniffs at the leather with too much interest.

"I couldn't think how else to not look like me," he complains. "Josh! It's so good to see you!"

"You too, Harry. Who's this lovely little fella?"

"This is Perky. Technicolor gave him to me."

Josh makes friends with Perky, stroking his gray-black feathers, clearly painfully delighted to be interacting with a living creature as Perky paws at his hand with a wing-arm and makes friendly squeaks. I bite my lip. Fernanda would put Josh back in prison just for being in the same room with Harry, I bet. My belly goes cold at the thought. Maybe I should've insisted Harry didn't come today…

"Father Ben said something about Dad?" says Harry, his green eyes bright with hope.

But my heart sinks as I take in the grim expression on Josh's face.

"Yeah, but it's not hopeful, okay?" Josh says. "I'm hoping we might be able to find out what actually *happened* to your dad. You know, for certain who did it. That's all."

"Let's make a drink and settle down," says Father Ben. "Then Josh can explain it all."

I don't really wanna wait and Harry fidgets impatiently, but I turned the water boiler on when I arrived so it doesn't actually take more than a minute to make four cups of Joe.

Josh sets his in front of him like he's gonna forget to drink it and glances from Harry to me.

"Okay, so in prison I made friends with a guy called Wilhelm." Pain flits across his face.

"Oh, West mentioned that Father Ben said that Jason had killed a friend of yours," I say. "Was that him? I'm really sorry."

"Weren't your fault, it were Jason's. Anyway, when Wilhelm were dying, he told me some stuff. Wilhelm were co-owners with a nasty piece of work called Seb, y'see. Seb got into debt and took the job to kill your dad to make a quick buck. A city-guy hired him to make it look like an animal attack."

My breath catches, hearing it so quick and bald like that. "Your friend's co-owner? That's who did it?"

"I wish it were that simple. Seb took the money to

do it, but once they had your dad, Wilhelm remembered—"

"Hang on," interrupts Harry. "Your friend was *there*?"

Josh bites his lip. "Yeah, Wilhelm were there. He were totally under Seb's thumb. Practically unable to think for himself, make decisions for himself. So yeah, he went along with it. Didn't wanna, but he did 'cause that's what he were like. And he were real, real sorry, if that makes any difference at all. But, anyway, thing is, Wilhelm had heard some country-guy saying he wanted to kill your dad. So to try and dodge the dirty job and give your dad a tiny chance, he suggested to Seb that they sell your dad to this guy and get paid twice. Seb liked the idea of that, so that's what they did.

"So the facts are, Seb and Wilhelm snatched your dad and sold him to a man who swore he were gonna kill him. But they didn't see him die. *But*, it's been almost two years, so clearly…" Josh swallows, his face softening as he glances from Harry to me. "Clearly," he finishes, very gently, "the country-guy did do it."

"Who?" I demand. "*Who*, Josh?"

Josh sighs, exchanging a look with Father Ben. *What?*

"Okay, the city-guy is called Martin Selman."

"Who?" says Harry blankly.

"*Selman*?" My stomach feels like it's gone into free fall. "Not…Carol's *brother*? The realtor?"

"Yeah. Father Ben confirmed that by checking the city records. Your step-mom's brother hired Seb for the hit. Guess she never thought to mention to him that she wouldn't inherit the farm, despite having married your dad. And the country-guy..." Josh hesitates again.

"Tell us, Josh!"

"Maurice Carr."

HARRY

"No!" I gasp, then hastily ease my grip on Perky when he wriggles in protest at my too-tight hands.

"That's *impossible*!" says Darryl, just as heated as I feel myself. "This Wilhelm guy was feeding you a line, Josh!"

"He weren't lying," says Josh. "Your neighbor, Maurice Carr, bought your father from Seb."

"But there's no motive!" Darryl protests, before I can find any words. "Mau and Dad are...were...best friends from childhood!"

Yeah, exactly!

But Josh and Father Ben exchange another look. My heart sinks, tightens, in anticipation.

"Maurice were supposed to be your guardian, right?" says Josh.

"Yeah?" From Darryl's expression, her heart is doing similar things.

"So where does he fall in the chain of…uh… inheritance? For the farm? He's in there. Ain't he?"

Darryl stays silent this time. So…

"Inheritance?" I echo stupidly, stroking Perky's soft gray feathers in absent-minded apology. Josh sounds so *certain*.

Darryl's face closes, like she's feeling nauseous. Her eyes get almost a…a scared look. "Mau comes after Harry," she says, her voice thin, but then strengthening. "Josh, what you're implying, that's impossible. Even assuming for one moment that Mau could kill Dad, to inherit he'd have to kill me and Harry too. He wouldn't do that, Josh! He couldn't!"

"I wouldn't underestimate what greed can do to a man," said Father Ben quietly, a grim look in his eye. I guess he has to listen to *everything*, in confession. But…

"I don't believe it!" Darryl voices the thought in my mind. "He hasn't made the slightest move against Harry or me in all this time. And he's been looking after that farm for a totally modest return for almost two years! That's not the actions of a man so deranged with greed he'd kill his best friend and his own wards! Is it?"

Josh purses his lips. "Sure, the lack of any further move against you and Harry is strange—thank God, because you'd never have been expecting it. But lack of suitable opportunity seems explanation enough. First you were with me, then after we were captured you were in-city, where your deaths would hardly have been ignored. And the facts remain. Maurice bought your dad from Seb, and your dad ain't been seen since."

"According to this Wilhelm!" I jump in fiercely. "Who sounds like a heap of no good!"

"He could've been lying, Josh," Darryl says earnestly. "Maybe they had some beef with Maurice and are trying to get him in trouble."

Josh shakes his head again. "Wilhelm were dying and he knew it. Knew he were about to stand before God and explain himself. He weren't lying. I'd stake my life on it."

"And I would have staked my life on being able to…to trust Mau with my life," whispers Darryl.

So would I. I stare at Darryl, at her pasty expression. "You don't…you don't actually believe this, do you?"

I mean…it's Uncle Mau. He's always been there for me—for us—the whole fifteen years of my life. I remember the time he found me all upset after Mom died, and put me on his shoulders and galloped me all around the farm for ages until I cheered up. I remember him taking Darryl and me *and* my riding orni to the rodeo along with his kids and their ornis more than once because Dad couldn't get away from the farm. I remember…

"It can't be Uncle Mau," I whisper. *Don't let it be*

Uncle Mau… My insides *hurt* at the thought.

"Maurice Carr were the last person known to have your dad," says Josh, unrelentingly. "What he did with him is what we don't know and need to find out. We'll probably have to confront him, but, well, Father Ben, how did you do?"

"At what?" I ask, trying to push away the pain inside, and putting Perky down on the floor so I can concentrate.

Father Ben takes a handful of tiny objects from his pocket. "I called in on Maurice on my way down south as soon as Josh told me about this. I've done that now and then since what happened—to check how he is. Him having lost his best friend and all that." Father Ben's mouth puckers as though he's bitten something sour.

"Anyway," Father Ben continues, "he's always welcoming enough so I knew it wouldn't rouse any suspicion. While I was there I stuck these trackers that I got from West onto all of his vehicles. And on the way back here just now I popped in again and retrieved them. So we can see where he's been going, which should fairly conclusively eliminate the infinitesimal possibility that—"

He breaks off abruptly and sighs.

Oh. That Dad's alive and still being held somewhere. My gut clenches even more painfully. It's what I want more than anything in the world—but I know there isn't really any chance at all. Not by now.

Josh holds out his hand for the trackers. "Let's take a look."

It's a quick enough job for him to link them to the main console and upload their data. Soon a map of the Carr farm is on the screen, covered in snaking multicolored lines.

"Darryl?" Josh says. "Can you help interpret this?"

She bends over the screen, tracing the colors. "That's the road truck. That one…dunno."

"Bentley has a truck now," says Father Ben.

"Right. Tractors…and that's Mau's farm truck." She taps the color that circles the farm the most.

"Anything look outta the ordinary?"

Darryl starts selecting one color at a time, studying the patterns. I peer over her shoulder. "Road truck's totally normal," she says. "Bentley's truck, too. Tractors…can't see anything strange." Frustration tinges her voice, and I know how she feels. I stare at the lines too, hunting for something, *anything*.

"Farm truck…" Her finger traces the mess of lines. "Normal over here. And here. And driving the fence… Driving the pastures… Hang on. What's this?" She taps where lines lead off the map, over and over again, then moves the map, following them further away from the main part of the farm. "Here." She taps the screen again, then inspects the part of the map now showing. "Circling something, twice, every single day."

"Buildings," says Josh, "according to the map, so I'd guess a fence inspection." He taps at the info, scrolling through. "Most days he doesn't just circle those buildings, he stops there for a while. At least once every two days, usually daily. Stays for some time. What is that place, Darryl? Harry? Do you know?"

I reach in past Darryl and zoom the map out again, checking the position of the buildings Uncle Mau is visiting so often. "I didn't even know there was a fence out there. Not the kind that needs checking daily."

"There's an old dwelling there," says Darryl. "From pre-Rewilding. Mau used to talk about pulling it down or at least taking the front off and putting a wide door on it so it could be used properly for farm storage. But he's never done anything with it."

And now he's going there every day? My heart lurches with hope.

Father Ben clearly sees my expression. "Now, let's not get ahead of ourselves. Those are buildings that belong to Maurice, on his own land. What innocent reasons could he have for going there regularly? Maybe he is finally converting it to storage."

"Not single-handedly." Darryl's nose wrinkles doubtfully. "Not day after day. And visiting just morning and evening, that's checking a habitation fence, that is."

"Could he have made himself a man cave?" persists Father Ben.

"He's already got one at the bottom of the yard," says Darryl. "So, another, theoretically, but it's unlikely."

"Vacation rental?" suggests Josh.

Darryl's face falls and my heart sinks along with it. "That's…slightly more likely, I suppose. I'm surprised he would actually stop there every day, though. You'd think he'd just check the fence and leave the tourists to enjoy their private retreat."

"Depending on exactly who's been there these last few weeks," points out Josh. "Mebbe they're chatty."

"Well, if he's managed to continuously let out a vacation cottage at this time of year I'm impressed," says Darryl, checking the data again. "And Josh is right, he hasn't missed a day. Anyway, he used to knock vacation rentals, used to say there was no way he'd have city-folk flapping around on his farm for no money."

"People can change their tune, if money gets tight or they just…well, change their mind," says Father Ben.

"True." Darryl draws a deep breath. "And I guess he could've turned his man-cave over to Bentley and made a new one or…well, there could be many explanations. But we've gotta check it, right? I already arranged three days off work in case we needed to investigate anything, since it's not easy to get at short notice with my job. We can go, right?"

"Yeah," says Josh. "But Father Ben's right. Don't get your hopes up. Why would he be keeping your dad there, for almost two years? It don't make no kinda sense."

Despite his words, my heart's pounding, though I have to make a quick grab for Perky who's getting interested in the leather dress again. "Can we go right away?"

"Whoa, whoa, wait up," says Darryl. "Harry, you can't come."

"What?" Dismay explodes inside me. "It's *Dad*!"

"If they catch Josh taking you out-city, they'll throw him back in jail for sure. You shouldn't even be *here*."

"But it's *Dad*!" Now I'm getting angry.

"Or a vacation rental."

"He didn't mention anything," Father Ben says, sounding thoughtful. "If he had a new enterprise underway, he's not the type to keep it under his hat. I agree that there's probably a perfectly innocent explanation, but I'm not convinced it's that."

"Well, the only way to find out is to go and look," I protest, putting Perky on my shoulder. "You've got to let me come, Ryll!"

"And what about when Susannah and Philip report you missing?"

"My foster parents," I answer Josh's blank look. "I can say I'm sleeping over with a friend for the weekend. They allow me plenty of freedom now. It won't even be a lie!"

Josh taps his fingers against the console thoughtfully. "It would actually be better to get over there today. Maurice usually makes his longer visit to the place in the morning, so we need to be cammed up and ready for him, with a plan. Or tomorrow evening, ready to make our move the following morning."

"We can't wait that long!" I protest. "Not now that we…that we know!"

"I doubt it would make any difference, after all this time," says Father Ben. "But if I'm coming on this expedition—and I think I should—then the sooner the better. I've still got a backlog of work from—well, you know."

Darryl scowls. "Look, I'm all for getting out there as quickly as possible. But as far as whether Harry comes…I think that has to be up to Josh."

JOSH

I know Darryl's trying to help by handing me the decision, but part of me wishes she'd just said Harry couldn't come. Spared me the risk. The thought of getting thrown straight back in prison… On the other hand, an extra gun would come in handy when it comes to confronting Maurice. And if it were my dad—heck, it would kill me to stay behind.

"Harry can come, as long as he thinks his cover will hold, and as long as he does *exactly* what he's told getting in and outta the city gates."

Harry nods earnestly, though he adds an indignant, "I always do what I'm told!"

Since that's almost completely true, I let it go.

"Okay, let me check the 'Vi over, and we'll hit the road. We can work on a few possible plans while we drive."

It'll take four hours to get to the Franklyn-Carr neck of the woods.

I must've sounded slightly unenthusiastic because Darryl gives me a searching look.

"Are you *sure*, Josh?"

"Yeah. It's your dad. This is the last chance. If he ain't there—and honestly, I don't expect him to be—about all we can do is try to guilt or startle a confession from Maurice, on or off record. I've been thinking about it, and I don't see what else there is to be done."

If he were a hunter, what we've got is enough to get him tried, but hunter trials are very different than city ones.

"Harry, you'd better check with Susannah about your sleepover," says Darryl. "I'll put together some bunks so we don't have to waste time on that later. Uh," she hesitates, clearly remembering she don't live in the 'Vi no more, "if that's what you want me to do, Josh?"

"Yeah, that's a good idea."

I open up the engine compartment and inspect everything—oil and coolant and battery are ready to go, *thanks, Technicolor*—then get out and circle the 'Vi, get underneath and everywhere, checking for corroded parts, but it's been well looked after, oiled and wrapped up, and nothing's wrong.

When I'm done, Father Ben unlocks his van so I can get my things. I open my cardboard box and slip the bagged urn inside so I can take it on board more discreetly.

Yeah, I'm glad Father Ben didn't let me waltz in there carrying it earlier.

What's that, Josh?

Oh, just the man partly responsible for killing your father…

Thank you, Father Ben.

DARRYL

It feels unreal to be back in the 'Vi, laying out sleeping bags and cramming stuff from a lower cupboard-bunk into other cupboards so Father Ben will have a berth tonight. But so good. So *right*.

The thought that in a couple of days I'll be back in-city, having to avoid Josh…it brings a painful lump to my throat.

Unless we find Dad. That would change every-thing. But the hope is sluggish in my chest. Josh and Father Ben are right. It's quite obvious Maurice didn't buy Dad to save his life. And if he did kill Dad—and however hard it is to believe, it seems near certain after all this time—has he just been biding his time until Harry and I go out-city again? And then he would have arranged some kinda accident for us, too?

Unbearable thought.

Josh comes back in with a cardboard box that yields a small quantity of mostly dull prison posses-sions. He takes out a set of devastatingly ordinary looking 'rocks' that look more like broken off corners of concrete than real stones. The only distinguishing feature about them is the letters carved into them. But he fastens them securely to the top of the picture frame with sticky pads, just in front of his precious blue raptor feather, like he values them a lot—then tucks a heavy gift bag carefully into the back of a cupboard. Leaving presents?

"You've lost your 'a,' Josh," says Harry, peering at the rocks, which spell j o s h u.

"I ain't got an a," he replies, trying to fend Harry away from the box, but Harry's grabbed a couple of Polaroid prints.

"Are you allowed cameras in prison?" he asks, peering at the pics.

"Polaroids only," Josh says. "So you have to mail the images in hard copy, not digital."

"So, who are these guys?"

"Cellmates. Other hunters."

There's a wariness to his voice that makes me move to look at the prints too. The top photo shows Josh with a tall, boney Native American older guy, a fractionally younger, more angular white guy, and... I peer more closely.

"*Misfire*, is that *Caleb*?"

"Huh?" Harry leans in closer as well, eyes widening.

"Yeah, he were still there when I left."

"And you wanted him in the picture?" Harry sounds outraged—Caleb did, after all, threaten to feed him to the rexes.

"Not particularly." There's a sharper edge to Josh's voice now. "But there were a real good reason why I weren't gonna exclude him, neither."

Harry flips to the other photo. Josh and another stranger are posing for the camera, grinning, each with one arm around the other's shoulders, the other hand holding up a pen. The guy's pale-skinned face contrasts with Josh's darker tan skin, but despite the hint of chubbiness in the guy's cheeks his arms are seriously muscular. His blond hair has an unexpectedly Afro curl to it. Happy eyes—blue, like mine—stare out. Across the white strip at the bottom of the picture is written in neat cursive: Hunter Two Fancy Writing Ltd.

"And who's this?" I demand. There's an edge to my voice that I didn't mean to be there.

Josh hesitates, then takes the photo from Harry before replying. "That's Wilhelm. We were cellmates for quite a while. Kept ourselves busy teaching guys cursive—or writing cards for 'em, fancy-like. A grateful customer gave us this."

"And you're gonna keep it?" demands Harry.

"Yeah," says Josh in a very even tone. "I'm gonna keep it." And he slips it into his pocket, like he doesn't trust Harry near it.

I understand how Harry feels—but I pause and try to see it from Josh's perspective. He was friends with this guy for months. Cellmates. They obviously got along. Probably made a horrible place nicer, having a friend around. And only then did he find out about…Dad. Can we really expect Josh to just forget everything that happened before?

Harry's glaring daggers at Josh's pocket, though.

I glance at Father Ben as something drops back into my mind. "Hang on, West said Father Ben said something about the guy getting killed protecting you from Jason?"

"Basically, yeah."

So Dad's gone 'cause of Wilhelm, but without him Josh would be dead? How confusing can a thing be?

"Well, that's good, at least." I try not to sound too grudging.

Josh's face eases a lot, his eyes lighting up. "Oh, and the other good thing is—I shoulda said already—I were able to tell Wilhelm you forgave him, before he died. Since you two couldn't be there."

Dead silence greets his words. Father Ben bites his lip, his eyes darting from me to Harry. Josh just smiles like he's told us something we'll be happy to hear. Harry gawps at him. I'm staring too, my mind frozen up.

Josh. Told. One. Of. The. Guys. Who. Killed. Dad. That. We. *Forgave.* Him?

What.

The.

Heck.

"You did *what*?" yells Harry, so loudly that Perky leaps from his shoulder onto the table, landing lightly on his two little clawed feet.

The smile slides from Josh's face, his eyes pinching anxiously. "I, uh, I pledged him you and Darryl's forgiveness. Since you weren't…y'know…there to…to tell him yourself."

"Tell him ourselves?" bellows Harry. "Why the heck would you think we'd want to *tell him ourselves*? He took Dad! Good as killed him! I'm *glad* he's dead, you hear? I'm glad, and you *lied,* 'cause I don't forgive him, not ever!"

He lunges toward the side door, but just in time I snap out of my paralysis and hit the override on the main console. "Harry, no!" He's not in his dress.

When the door won't open, he spins around and goes up the ladder to the turret, fast as a hungry rodo climbing a tree after a songbird, slamming the hatch down with a massive clang that reverberates deafeningly around the 'Vi. *Click.* He locks it. Perky cowers from the noise, his little wing-limbs tucked to his chest.

Father Ben's gaze shifts back to me. So does Josh's, his brow wrinkled with dismay, though his hands reach out automatically to soothe the little 'saur.

I close my eyes tight, the only way to hide from their eyes. I take slow deep breaths, fighting not to start yelling myself. Fighting to…to just not. Not *do* anything. Not *say* anything. Not immediately. I don't… don't trust myself to do so.

"I…" I open my eyes again.

Josh stares at me, his eyes wide and hopeful as a puppy, looking more his old self for a moment.

"I…" The words come out strangled. No, it's no good. "Excuse me," I choke, brushing past him and climbing swiftly up into the overCab berth that was always mine before, sliding the door closed behind me.

I curl up into a ball on the mattress, arms locked around my legs, face pressed to my knees, and shake— and sob, as quietly as I can.

The way Josh looked at me, the way he spoke

about it, like it never even occurred to him we wouldn't forgive. I feel like I'm letting him down.

And I'm furious with him. All at the same time.

I mean, how can he dismiss so lightly what Wilhelm did to Dad?

JOSHUA

I stare at Father Ben in dismay. "Did I...do something wrong?"

Father Ben heaves a big sigh. "No, of course not. You just...well, you probably could have told them about it more...tactfully."

"Tactfully? Ain't it...something to be happy about? I mean, he's *dead* now. They'll never get the chance."

"Josh, forgiveness is engrained very deeply in Hunter culture, thanks to Saint Des. Even the most deeply committed Catholics from other backgrounds may struggle to forgive quite so readily—especially when it's totally sprung on them. Quite honestly, they had enough to deal with today, without adding that into the mix."

"You think I shouldn't have said nothing?"

Father Ben shrugs. "Well, you needed to tell them sometime. It's done, anyway. Give them a minute to process it all."

Process it all? All *what?* He'd done them wrong, he were sorry, he needs to be forgiven. Ain't complicated. I shake my head slightly. Farmers ain't like city-folk, but sometimes even they confuse me.

With a sigh, I let the little rodo go, now he's calmer, and finish emptying my cardboard box, picking up a few things to move to my cab bedroom. Though, I guess, after this trip, I can have the Master Bedroom back since Darryl won't be here. What we find at the Carr farm won't change that, neither way. The thought makes my heart slump right down into my boots.

"Can we have Mass or Adoration tonight?" I ask Father Ben, going back into the living area.

"Both, if we've got everything organized in time for tomorrow."

My heart lifts. That'll make Darryl and Harry feel better, right? It'll sure make me feel better. However wonderful it is to see them, this day ain't turning out quite so celebratory as I expected.

I place my hand on the scanner of the gun cabinet and open it to check everything's still in there. But it is. The police don't seem to have taken nothing. Guess my firearms had no bearing on the case whatsoever. Darryl and Harry's rifles are safe in there too. I take mine out and strip it, start cleaning it real good.

If it comes down to Maurice Carr or one of us, it

ain't gonna be one of us just 'cause my rifle jams at the wrong moment!

DARRYL

Shamelessly eavesdropping on the conversation between Josh and Father Ben only makes me feel worse, because Father Ben clearly thinks Josh did something good.

I mean, my head *knows* that he did.

But my heart…aches. Tomorrow it's almost certainly gonna be confirmed, finally, that Dad is dead. Any last tiny shreds of hope will be gone. Forgiving one of the people responsible for his death tonight feels like…like kicking Dad in the teeth.

And yet…the image of the smiling guy from the photo creeps back into my head. When Josh obviously cares so much, it's hard not to see Wilhelm as a person. *He were real, real sorry*, that's what Josh said. Did it matter to him, then? About being forgiven?

Josh obviously considers this Seb guy to be far more responsible. At least no one's asking me to forgive *him* right now, today. Surely I can manage the reluctant flunkey?

Dad's faith was always real important to him. He tried to pass that on to Harry and me. He'd want us to forgive, I know he would.

I've just gotta do it.

HARRY

I stare out at the 'Vi-park without seeing it, knowing I'm safely invisible behind the polarized windows of the turret.

How *dare* Josh forgive that murderous thug on my behalf! What did he think he was *doing*? You can't just…just do that, just forgive someone in some else's name!

Guess hunters think they can.

Well, I'm not a hunter! And I don't want to be a hunter. Least of all if it means forgiving filth like this Wilhelm.

How could Josh *smile* while he told us what he'd done? Like he thought we'd be, what, *happy*? If this Wilhelm guy was still alive, I'd like to…to punch him in the face, bare minimum. He deserved what he got from Jason! I'd have let him die without a word of comfort.

I shift my shoulders as my gut clenches uncomfortably.

Would I? If I'd actually been sitting there, beside a dying man?

Well…maybe…maybe I wouldn't have been *mean* to him. But to *forgive* him, like what he did to Dad was nothing?

What he did to Dad was everything.

What he did to Dad *destroyed* everything.

It's different for Darryl, I guess. Coming to the 'Vi brought her to a lifestyle she loves. For me, it was just better than being in-city.

I want Dad back. I want to go home.

I know Father Ben would say I should forgive. But how can I forgive the guy who took those things from me? Has he given them back to me? Made amends? I don't think so! I'm stuck in-city with nothing but bullying and smog to look forward to. With no idea when—if—Darryl will even get custody of me so we can go home.

Home. Next door to Uncle Mau. Who killed Dad.

Did he?

Josh seems so sure. Darryl's convinced. So is Father Ben.

I don't want it to be true, but it makes sense of everything. Finally, there's an obvious motive.

Martin Selman, Seb, Wilhelm…and Uncle Mau.

They all killed Dad.

Fury builds, a painful heat in my veins, like my blood is boiling.

Uncle Mau killed Dad.

They. All. Killed. Dad.

The vehicle shifts slightly, the familiar movement of someone climbing down from the master bedroom bunk. Darryl? Did she climb up there while I wasn't paying attention?

Quickly, I press the button on the intercom so I can

hear what's said in the main living area. Surely she won't forgive Wilhelm? Won't betray Dad?

Will she?

JOSHUA

The familiar cleaning routine soon soothes my jittery stomach—and even makes a start on my nine months of prison memories. Despite regular pauses to give Perky some attention—he's a real friendly little fella—my rifle's almost back together when Darryl finally slides the door open and climbs down from her berth. Warily, I watch as she steps over to the table.

"Uh, Josh?"

"Yeah?"

She swallows; bites her lip for a moment. "Uh…thank you for forgiving Mr. Fenn on my behalf."

The tension eases from my body. "No problem. What else would I have done?"

She grimaces. "Probably good it happened this way. I don't know if I coulda…coulda risen to the occasion, as it were."

"Huh?"

"Darryl just means, all's well that ends well," says Father Ben.

"Oh. Yeah."

"So, uh, how do we get Harry past the gates?" Darryl asks.

"He puts Trudy's dress back on," I grin. "He's under eighteen so he don't need no ID." I glance at her. "What about you? What will it mean for you getting custody if there's a record of you being in my company? 'Cause I don't think you can get away with claiming to be under-eighteen no more, even if you wanted to lie which I'm sure you don't."

"Will they know how many people are in the vehicle?" she asks. "Can't I just hide in the back?"

"They have heat scanners," I say. "Guys who smuggle stuff rig up hidden and heat-shielded compartments, but I ain't got none of those. The freeze-drier would block the thermal scanners, but if they find you—or Harry—in there, it makes it totally clear we're up to something we shouldn't be."

"Hmm." She settles into a seat beside me, turning her face away from Father Ben as though almost trying to exclude him from the conversation. "Well, one question is, what are we gonna do next? I mean, assuming there's no sign of Dad. If we confront Mau, we'll probably get some idea from how he behaves if...if it really is true. But unless we can tape a confession—and I don't reckon he'd fall for that—what hope do we have of bringing him to trial? Could, uh...could a hunter court do anything?"

I shake my head. "He's a farmer. Not a hunter. Hunter justice is strictly dealt out to hunters only. Don't matter what someone's done. If they ain't a hunter, they ain't gonna be touched."

"Once we confront him, he'll know we know."

"Yeah. Almost makes me wonder if—" I break off.

"If what?"

"If we should," I say. "Except…"

"If we don't, we'll never know for sure?"

"Yeah."

"But if we do, we risk him coming after us more openly," Darryl muses. "To shut us up."

"Yep."

"And then there's Carol's *misfiring* excuse for a brother. How do we touch him?"

"We can't. Unless the police got Seb to cut a deal to save his own hide, but I ain't convinced Martin Selman's going down just because one hunter—and one with a criminal record already—*claims* he paid him to do something."

"It's your word, too."

"My word about something Wilhelm told me. Which Wilhelm can never corroborate. And I have a criminal record too."

"Wilhelm didn't tell anyone else, ever?"

"The prison chaplain. In confession."

"Oh. Well, that's no use."

Darryl finally glances at Father Ben. "Do you think there's any hope? That we could bring any of them to justice?"

Father Ben sighs. "Very doubtful. Josh is right.

There are no witnesses. No proof."

"But," says Darryl slowly, "I'm not sure it really makes much difference if we confront Mau or not. How can we go back to the farm and just live there next door to him, knowing what we know?"

Her queasy expression lurches between anger and deep uncertainty. I don't envy her dilemma. Now that Darryl's eighteen and can make a new will, there'll be no motive for Mau to hurt them if they keep quiet and pretend they don't know what he did to their dad—but there's also no closure for them. But...

"Mebbe it *would* be best not to confront him," I say doubtfully. "At least that way you could safely go home."

"No, they can't," says Father Ben firmly. "Don't you see? It doesn't matter if Maurice knows they know or not. It doesn't matter if they're no credible threat to him. They'll never be safe near him because of his guilty conscience. They cannot go home, not while he's there."

DARRYL

My heart plummets, a sick feeling settling in my stomach.

Father Ben continues, clearly keen to make sure I'm convinced, "The only way Maurice can feel safe after doing what he's done is to silence anyone who might point the finger at him. If you were back on the farm, even if you were living there as though nothing had happened, eventually, he'd strike, believing it would bring him peace of mind. Probably it would only throw him deeper into fear and paranoia and, one hopes, guilt. But, be that as it may, he'd likely do it thinking it would help."

My fists clench on my braid, pulling too hard. "Anyway, to just *live* there, letting him get away with it! But to live *anywhere*, knowing what he's done and doing nothing!"

The hatch squeaks up and Harry's head pops down. "Can't we just put a bullet in the scumbag?" he snarls, scowling at me and Josh like he's almost too mad to speak.

Clearly he's been listening on the intercom system.

Considering how rough Hunter justice is reputed to be, I'm surprised how shocked Josh looks at the suggestion. "We can't do that!" he exclaims.

"Why not?" demands Harry, as Perky springs onto the ladder and races up to him. "If we know he's guilty, and it's the only way there'll be justice?"

"Because we don't have the right," says Josh patiently. "Without that, it *can't* be justice."

"Josh is correct," says Father Ben, very quellingly. "Vigilante assassinations are not justice. If we can't work out how to get justice in this life, we will have to leave it to the Lord. Which means Maurice will probably get double punishment in the next life, so there's no need to be too down-hearted about that."

Harry scowls at him for that, all the same.

"But if we can't go back to the farm," I say, my voice very soft as I meet Josh's eyes, "then…"

JOSHUA

Darryl trails off, but I hear the end of her thought.

…then why stay in-city any longer?

My heart lifts. After we confront Maurice, she wants to run, doesn't she? Skip into Yoming or Kota, the three of us, live free. But she don't dare suggest it, 'cause the consequences for me—and probably her, too—will be so bad if we get caught.

Probably better not to talk about it in front of Father Ben, neither. He won't be prepared to lie about anything he overhears, and we don't want him locked up again because of us.

Despite the risks, my heart feels a hundred times lighter all of a sudden. Mebbe I won't have to leave Darryl and Harry in-city and drive away, not see them for months or even years. Mebbe we can be together, a family again.

"But what about that city-rat?" demands Harry, too fixated on the justice issue to have followed our train of thought. "And that Seb guy?"

"Same thing applies," says Father Ben. "And

Selman has received some punishment already, after a fashion, losing his sister. I doubt that was part of his plan."

"Yeah," I say, "And Seb we are not going nowhere near, you understand? We cannot make one move against *him* unless we're sure we have him stone cold."

Has he had his letter yet, telling him I'm now his co-owner? Bet he just loves that. No, I ain't going nowhere near him, ever, if I can help it. Fortunately his usual patch is far to the south-east of Exception state. I remember Wilhelm saying they'd never even been to Exception City—until Seb brought them here to look for that shady job he wanted, clearly. Our paths should never cross.

"Anyway, first things first," I say. "Let's get out to the Carr farm, check the one anomaly, then we can confront Maurice, since it seems it won't make no difference neither way. And then we can think what to do next."

I catch the glance Darryl shoots my way, and my heart warms, quickens with excitement. Yeah, she thinks we should skip. So do I. Except…the way I've been thinking about Darryl these days, should I really be going off with her like that?

But it's not like we'll be alone. Harry will be with us. It'll be just like before.

Right, Saint Des?

In the end, I sit in the cab with the others and hand my ID to the gate guard along with Josh and Father Ben's cards. Father Ben says nothing, though he must guess which way our minds are working. Why let the authorities keep us in-city with Harry as their hostage for several more years if we can't even safely return to the farm after that anyway? And the very worst thing that could happen right now, today, would be the guards finding me hidden in the freeze-drier and stopping us. Stopping us from finally finding out once and for all who killed Dad. Like Harry, now that we're so close, I can't bear any delay.

As the gate guard hands me back the IDs and we drive on, I know we've just burned our bridges to the ground behind us—but all I feel is relief. Is Fernanda going to be notified that I left the city? Or that Josh did? Does she have grounds to set up something like that? I'm over eighteen and out of her control, but Josh— Josh is out on parole. If she's got tabs on anyone, it's probably him.

But she'll be expecting him to be leaving city today, right? So the real question is, can she access the information about who left with him?

Never mind. It's not today it will come back to bite me. Today, we're out on the highway and clear away. It's only when I try to get custody of Harry.

And it looks like we won't be troubling the city authorities about that after all.

HARRY

My mind's so full of murderous scumbags—Maurice, Carol's brother, Seb, Wilhelm—that we've driven for some way before it registers what Darryl did back there. I open my mouth—then shoot Father Ben a look. And close it again.

Darryl doesn't care about being seen with Josh. That means after we're done with Mau, we're not coming back. I guess we'll have to drop Father Ben off somewhere safe—and then we're heading out-state.

A hint of guilt stirs, at the thought of how worried Susanna and Philip will be when I don't come back from my 'sleepover.' But excitement and relief surge through me far more strongly. Susanna and Philip have been letting me homeschool this semester—but they still keep making noises about putting me back in school after Christmas. I don't need to worry about that anymore! Ironically, I guess I can thank Murderous Mau for that. Knowing we can't safely return home changes everything, doesn't it?

Or maybe, despite all the sensible things Darryl has been saying for months, it would always have happened this way. She and Josh snapping back together like two powerful magnets, impossible to re-separate without immense force.

Well, I'm sure not complaining. My mood lifts so much that even my anger at her for forgiving Wilhelm eases a little.

"Look." Darryl points, her voice calm but her eyes alight with joy.

To one side of the highway, a large herd of triceratops are grazing at a safe distance. *You've been working with 'saurs every day*, I almost say. *Why are you so excited?* But seeing them in the zoo just isn't the same, is it?

Oh, yeah, that's right. We're unSPARKed again, for the first time in nine months. Guess I should be keeping watch for danger. Oops.

I sit up straighter and start scanning the roadside, the horizon, checking the mirrors and the rear-view screen in a steady routine, the way Father Ben and Darryl are doing, keen to prove that I haven't turned into a city-boy.

"Are you gonna get Kiko from Mau?" I ask eventually, stroking Perky, who's napping in my lap as we cruise along the flat, level highway, a herd of wild edmos falling behind us. So far we haven't seen anything more dangerous than a juvenile allo. Some of the smallest cars did pull over, remaining stationary as they waited for the large carni'saur to move away from the road. But our armor is allosaur-proof. No need to stop.

"Yeah," says Darryl. "It may make a good excuse for being there, depending on how it all goes down."

"I suggest we keep Maurice at the point of a rifle from the earliest possible moment," says Josh grimly, his eyes flicking smoothly between the road ahead and the mirrors and the surrounding area without any pause. "Collecting Kiko ain't a good enough excuse to explain you being out-city, let alone with me, let alone with *Harry*. He's gonna guess we're onto him. And you can't trust him, okay?"

"He's not the man we thought we knew," adds Father Ben grimly. "That man doesn't exist. Be very careful, you two."

My anger at Uncle Mau fades again, seesawing me back into disbelief. How can you know someone your whole life and be this wrong about them?

"I will," I mutter.

"Josh, you'd better be the one whose job it is to keep a gun on him absolutely all the time," says Darryl. "He might bet on me or Harry hesitating. But not you."

"Let's *please* try not to let *anyone* get shot," says Father Ben. "Including Maurice. Okay?"

"No matter the provocation," Josh backs Father Ben up. "The only reason he gets a hole in him is if it's necessary to protect ourselves. Understood?"

For some reason he looks very hard at me. I glower back.

"*Understood?*"

It's Josh's 'Vi. Feeling hunter discipline closing around me again after all these months in-city is a slight shock. I mean, city-folk love the word 'no,' but they always couple it with opportunities to 'express yourself' and explanation after explanation, until they're convinced you 'understand'—and preferably agree, too. But I know Hunter rules well enough to know that Josh won't hesitate to lock my rifle up and make me go without it if he isn't satisfied I'm going to follow orders.

"Understood," I say firmly.

"Good." Josh jerks his head toward the dash screen without taking his hands from the wheel. "Darryl, you know the area. Take a look on the terrain map and find us a good vantage of that mystery building, and plot a discreet route to take us to it."

JOSHUA

While we're on the main highway we catch-up on what we've been up to for the last almost-year. Only the very most basic news has been filtering to me in prison via Darryl and Harry's neighbors. Father Ben was allowed to see them, and also me, while my friends from Technicolor 'Vi were allowed to see them and also Darryl and Harry. *Everyone still alive and well* has been about the extent of it.

"The zoo?" I soon exclaim. "Do you know Ned

Greyson?"

"My boss," says Darryl, grinning. "I work in the carni'saur department. He was so thrilled when he heard you'd trained me that he offered me a job on the spot. I'll be sorry to—" She breaks off abruptly.

Sorry to disappoint him by quitting so abruptly? Hopefully he'll take it in stride. Though it's not like I'm gonna be supplying 'saurs to Exception Zoo again no time soon, the way things are looking.

"How's Gold?" I ask, picturing the allosaur with her fine-looking golden crest feathers. How many years, now, since Uncle Z and I rescued her from the winter snow as a little chick and took her to a zoo? Even two years ago, she were already all-but-full-grown when I saw her on that *very* memorable occasion.

"Strong and healthy," says Darryl, with a smile. "Although, the other month, she ate a lapdog that some idiot smuggled into the zoo and accidentally dropped into her enclosure. I felt sorry for the dog— the owner, not so much. I mean, holding your pet over an allosaur paddock? Seriously?"

"I've seen worse than a dog held over an allosaur paddock," I say dryly.

"Yeah, I heard all about that. Absolutely hair-raising. Gold must really like you."

I shrug. "I just kept calm and gave her some good reasons not to chomp on me."

"You know there's a video on the net?" says Harry. "I hardly believed Darryl when she told me what Ned said you did to save that little girl, but then I watched it for myself."

"Really? Huh. I must remember that next time someone calls me a liar."

Though I don't normally bother telling that tale. No one ever believes me.

HARRY

"So, first we watch," I check, jiggling my knees up and down in a mixture of excitement and impatience, making Perky relocate to my shoulder. "See what he does while he's there? And when he's driving away…"

"We need to figure out some way to stop him," says Josh, his eyes not pausing their constant cycle. "Capture him, ideally."

We've been on the minor road that cuts through the hills to the farm for several hours now, seeing far more wildlife than on the main highway. We even had to stop briefly as a rex roamed nearby, and again for over twenty minutes waiting for a bull triceratops to get out of the road. Too large and dangerous a herbi'saur to simply try to shoo on its away. But we're nearly there. The familiarity of the passing landscape keeps bringing a lump to my throat. I can't believe we're almost home. Finally.

But we can't *stay*. That hurts worse than I expected.

I've been feeling so much happier since I realized we wouldn't be going back in-city, but my insides are starting to feel awfully tight and heavy. No more city is great—but unlike Darryl, long-term, I *want* to go back to the farm. I thought I only had to wait until I was eighteen. Ages, it felt like, but at least it was a definite date. Now… Now I've absolutely no idea when. Not until Mau's a harmless old man? But why should it be me who has to stay away when he's the one who's done something wrong?

But if we can't *prove* anything…it makes me helpless with fury and furious with helplessness.

"Whoa!" I slam into Darryl's shoulder as Josh spins the wheel, sending the huge vehicle careering down the bank beside the road. The back end pitches up violently, then the front end as we come level again. The pivoting double rear axles cope with the maneuver, but we're all thrown violently around. We'd have been better off if we'd had our off-road harnesses on instead of mere seatbelts.

"Am I the only one actually keeping watch?" demands Josh, pressing hard on the accelerator and throwing the vehicle into a sharp left hand turn as there's a violent thump nearby. "Been in the city too long, have we?"

My cheeks heat up. I weren't paying attention, and I know it. Too busy thinking about…everything.

"What is it?" I ask, craning to get a look in the mirrors just as Josh throws us sideways with another turn, then accelerates again as he tries to throw off whatever is chasing us.

"Testy steg bull."

Ugh, there it is! The big herbi'saur surges alongside, startlingly fast despite its comparatively short legs. The tips of the huge plates along its spine loom taller than our roof, but it's the thagomizer—the spikes at the end of its tail—that Josh is trying to avoid, I bet. Even as I watch, it swings at us again.

Josh throws us into another violent turn. Another thud as the thagomizer hits the dirt instead of us.

"It can't actually break in, right?" I say defensively.

"You ever tried to pry a three-foot steg tail spike outta your armor?" says Josh, aiming us toward a more open area where our superior speed can win out. It takes us further from the road, but the minor road here is too bumpy and twisting to win any races. "If it gets us, I'll be glad to let you take care of that."

Uh-oh. He will, too. Hunters are rather like farmers, they believe in learning through experience. Whereas city-folk would tell you in five different ways, probably including a full multimedia presentation, that getting a spike out would be hard, but never dream of letting you attempt any such thing.

"Argh, give up, you silly beast," mutters Josh, eyeing the rear view screen and keeping the gas pedal firmly down as we careen over the open ground. "We ain't a rival male, get that?"

"It's not even Christmas," I say. "It's not mating season yet, is it?"

"It is for stegs," says Josh. "First species to come into season. Very long egg gestation period. They lay around the same time as all the other species, in the spring, but they mate much earlier."

"Oh. Yeah, I remember." My cheeks get even hotter. Maybe I have been in-city too long. I'm sure Dad taught us that, years ago. I glance at Darryl, surprised she didn't volunteer the information, then turn toward her. "Darryl?"

Her face is really pale, kinda clammy looking, and she's staring straight ahead like she's not seeing the landscape.

"*Darryl?* Are you okay?"

DARRYL

I struggle to fight free of the memory, but every swerve throws me deeper into it…

Snapping on my safety catch, I drop my rifle tip to the floor and lean over to Carol again, grappling with her, trying to steer us at least slightly to the right. We've got to get back to the straight, flat road where we can outrun the raptors safely and easily!

A crunching sound, followed by a tinkling of glass as

Harry breaks the rear window, and suddenly I can hear the excited raptor chatter from behind us much more clearly. Carol's breathing in sobs, hunching lower and lower. I'm about to reach for my rifle again, unfasten my belt, and climb into the back to help Harry when I see what's ahead.

"NO, CAROL!" *I grab for the wheel, trying to steer us away from the crag-encircled bog we're heading straight toward. Carol fights me with deranged strength and from this angle I just can't hold on—the wheel jerks from my hands, spinning hard left, and the rear of the truck lifts...then we're rolling, gravity flips, my rifle butt smacks me in the jaw, Kiko screeches, Harry yells in pain...and with a squelching sound, we come to a halt, right side up, for a wonder.*

Much good that will do us. Dry rocky ground is visible just feet from my door, but we're in the bog. All four wheels...

+

"Darryl?" Harry's shaking my shoulder. "*Darryl?*"

+

...Anger and helplessness curdle inside me. I knew it wasn't safe traveling with Carol but...what else could I do? Guess I should've insisted she drop Harry at Mau's. Maybe that was the responsible thing to do. Or refused to go unless she let me drive? Too late now.

Too late.

Time to start dropping those raptors; see if we can put them off. Ignoring the cold voice telling me that there are simply too many of them, I'm just getting the lead Dakotaraptor—now only six hundred feet away—in my sights when a most unraptor-like roar fills the air and something huge and gray surges alongside, blocking my view. For a split second, my confused eyes take it for some sort of large herbi'saur—then I register the metallic finish and the shape. A HabVi!

The vehicle's side door hisses open and a voice shouts from the cab, "In, quick!"

I unsnap my seatbelt. "Harry, go!"

The door clicks and the truck rocks as Harry leaps out, but I'm too busy unfastening Carol's seatbelt. "Carol, come on!" She hasn't even moved!

Why is no one shooting from the 'Vi? I haven't heard anything, no sign we have cover!

"Hurry up!" yells the voice. "Raptors incoming, whaddah-ya-waiting-for!"

"Carol, hurry!" I pull on her arm as hard as I can. "Carol, look, it's safe in there, come on!"

She just clings to the steering wheel, rocking to and fro.

"Move, NOW!" comes the hunter's voice, vibrating with urgency. I'm taking too long…

"Carol, just follow me!" I fling the door open and leap from the truck…

+

"Darryl?" Josh's voice. Hands grip my shoulders, gentle but firm. "Darryl, come back to us. You're okay. It's not then."

"When?" Harry's voice.

"Some time bad," Father Ben hushes him.

+

"…IN!" I glimpse urgent eyes, a reaching hand, and hurl myself upwards, one foot pushing off the step, my hand seizing the extended one—a yank, and I tumble onto the driver's seat, tangled with my rescuer. Even as I land, I'm trying to sit up. We both turn, grabbing the door handle and heaving as hard as we can—too slow, a ruffled-looking raptor's head appears in the gap, lunging for us. The guy's foot shoots out, slamming into the raptor's nose with such force it jerks back.

We haul frantically on the door and it closes…almost. The raptor's got one wing-claw into the gap. It pulls, terrifyingly strong, and we cling on for dear life. Then, as it eases up for a moment, thinking alike, we both let the door swing open—just enough to give us the leverage to slam it hard…with a screech, the raptor snatches its wing-claw clear and with one more desperate heave, the door clicks shut.

Only then, panting, shaking, safe, I remember Carol.

"Carol!" I lunge for the door, but the guy touches a control and the lock snicks.

"It's too late!"

I raise my rifle, but my eyes make sense of the scene outside just in time to see the pack racing away into the shelter of the rocky outcrops, dragging…something.

"Carol! O God, Carol!"

+

...I'm sobbing. Sobbing and shaking. Josh's arms are around me. I burrow close against him, struggling to breathe.

"Carol…" I whisper. "*Carol…*"

"Oh." Harry sounds nauseous. "*Then.*"

What's wrong with me?

"I'm sorry," I whisper. "I've never… I've never done anything like this…"

"Shhhh." Josh just rubs my back soothingly. "You had a flashback. Ain't nothing you need to apologize for."

"But I've never, ever…

"Shhh. Just some'at that happens sometimes. I'm sorry my driving set it off."

I guess that's what it was. The first swerve, coming so totally unexpected, flung me right back.

"I left her," I whisper.

Harry takes the Lord's name in vain. "*Don't* start that again, Ryll! It wasn't your fault!"

Since Josh detaches an arm from me for a moment and Harry yelps, I guess Our Lord's honor has just been defended. Harry's been in-city too long, all right.

"It *weren't* your fault, Darryl," says Josh quietly, wrapping his arm around me again. "Your only chance to save her, there at the end, were to try to trigger herd instinct and make her follow you. Ain't your fault her instincts were too citified. It were still the only possible thing you coulda done."

"It wasn't enough."

"Never is, when you lose someone. Don't make it your fault."

I shelter against Josh for a little longer as my breathing slowly comes back under control. And my mind. I've been over and over this, since it happened. I've talked to Father Ben, in and out of confession. What happened to Carol wasn't my fault. I just wish I could convince my heart.

Finally, I manage to sit up properly and look around us. We're away from the place where we met the steg, up in craggy ground. Josh wouldn't have pulled over unless we'd left the angry beast behind us. I dry my eyes on my sleeve and lean to inspect the map.

"Okay, there's not much point trying to get back to the road, now." My voice sounds stuffed up, but I speak firmly. "We can start looping around this way." I point.

"Okay," says Josh, accepting my self-declaration of being recovered with a refreshingly un-cityish lack of argument. "Let's go."

HARRY

Everyone's quiet as we carry on our way. Josh is concentrating on the off-road driving. Darryl slumps tiredly, her face drawn, absent-mindedly stroking Perky, who's wormed his way under her hand. Father

Ben diligently inspects the surrounding landscape for danger, since he's the most alert out of us three passengers.

I try to keep watch too, but it's hard. I keep shooting looks at Ryll. I've never seen anything like what happened to her—except that panic attack Josh had that one time, when he first learned he might go to prison for helping us. That was a little similar, I guess.

Josh clearly knew what was wrong with Darryl at once. Obviously didn't think it was odd—or serious—just something needing sympathy and reassurance. Father Ben didn't seem too alarmed either—just sorry for her.

I guess that crazy ride was very like when Carol panicked and tried to get away from the raptors. Only, where we were then, if she'd simply gone back onto the nice straight road, not away from it, we'd have got away no problem.

Maybe that's another reason Darryl doesn't seem so interested in going back to the farm long-term. Maybe it would all remind her too much of Carol and Dad. Nah, if Fernanda had let us stay, the memories would have got overlain with new ones. Guess she just wants to be a hunter. Unlike me. In fact, I think the real reason is sitting beside me, driving.

Nah, that's not fair. Even if we could magically go home and Josh disappeared off and made it clear he wasn't interested, I don't reckon she'd stay. Not once I was grown-up. She's too in love with the wide open wilderness.

Not interested? Yeah right! They watch each other like they're each afraid the other is going to vanish if they look away.

Anyway, I can worry about the farm later. About wicked Wilhelm, and forgiveness, and everything.

Right now, we just need to find out what happened to Dad.

JOSHUA

Dawn finds all four of us up in the turret, ready and waiting. I had Harry shut Perky into Critter Cage One to ensure he can't slip out through an open window or cause a distraction at a key moment. We're parked behind a shielding outcrop of rock, just the turret poking higher and well covered in camo-netting. A small distant hill behind us prevents us from being silhouetted, but Maurice was born and bred on this farm. He'll know every inch of the landscape. If he looked hard, he'd probably spot us, despite our efforts. But he'd really have to be looking.

It's the best we can do, anyway.

We have a clear view down to the shallow valley Maurice drives along every morning and evening. The open end of the valley points out into Maurice's pastures and, if you go far enough, the main farm complex. The other end is closed off by minor crags, slightly before which stands the ancient house, which I'm currently inspecting through the telescopic sites of my rifle. Now that the sun is on it from this side, I can see it properly, unlike last night.

"For a pre-Rewilding house, that place is in real good repair," I say. "The roof looks perfect. Old-fashioned grilles on the windows, so I'm guessing they never upgraded to raptor-proof glass, and no shutters, neither. But the fence is perfect, too."

"Well, Maurice never let it fall down," Darryl says.

"Lot of undergrowth close to it, though," says Harry. "If it's touching—"

"I don't think it's touching," says Darryl. "Listen…" She reaches out and opens one of the turret windows, letting the dawn silence enfold us.

"Darryl's right." I wave at the wind gauge. "Wind's toward us. If all that undergrowth were touching the fence, we'd hear the sparking. I'd lay high odds a narrow strip just around the fence has been mown. Anyone looking at the place may assume it's a disused fence because of the overgrowth. But actually it's working perfectly. Old fence, no top lights—you'd have to go close to see the base lights. That could be chance—or could be a deliberate set-up for when you value your privacy. Interesting. I think Father Ben's right. It's looking more like a man-cave than a vacation rental."

"He's got four kids," says Darryl, "a nanny, and what, two workers, Father Ben?"

"No, he's got three, now. Took on another one shortly after partial responsibility for your farm landed on him."

"Another…" Her face falls. "Y'know, I think his father had a farm worker and his family living down there, for many years."

"You think the *worker's* living in it?" cries Harry, voice rising in dismay.

"That would make a whole lotta sense." Yeah, I'm sorry to have to say it, but this is likely the innocent explanation we've been looking for. "They're probably just not bothering to mow more ground than necessary. And it would be Maurice's responsibility to do the fence checks. If it's a senior worker, Maurice might be popping in most mornings to go over the plan for the day. It all fits. The worker's vehicle mebbe parked around the back where we haven't been able to get a good look. But we picked a spot well away from the place, in case there is someone there, so our plan should be okay."

Although it's cool this December morning, I carefully open all the windows on the valley side of the turret, making sure the camo-nets remain well-positioned. "Okay. Does everyone know what to do?"

"Yes," says Father Ben.

"Yep," says Harry.

Darryl nods silently.

"Good. Let's not mess this up. Because if we do, things could get very messy."

We have one chance to secure Mau and confront him safely.

HARRY

The wait is agony, and I have to try not to fidget like a little kid. Josh applies stake-out rules, which means staying silent. Sound travels so well at this time of day, and Uncle Mau usually makes his morning visit while doing his early check of the fence and pastures.

We've got a good plan. Clever, even. But it all hinges on Josh being able to make a very, very difficult shot. After nine months in prison.

I suggested he practice, but we haven't time to drive well out of earshot, aside from the risk of Maurice or any of the other people who live here noticing us roaming around his land. I said, couldn't Josh use the silencer for practice, too, but apparently it will only suppress one or two shots and then it has to be refilled. And he doesn't have any refill because he almost never uses it, and the stuff costs stupid money.

So he has to get it perfect, first time.

If he's nervous, he isn't letting on. He sits, still and quiet, watching, for all the world like he's waiting for a target animal to wander along. Which I guess we kinda are.

I eye the buildings. A worker house? It's painfully plausible, since Uncle Mau took on a new guy recently. If they're a private type, they might prefer to live out here...

Well, we'll know soon enough.

Come on Maurice, you murdering monster.

We want to have a little chat with you.

DARRYL

Josh has set up the sniping board, so he'll be able to lie flat, level with the window, to make the shot. For now, he sits in a chair to avoid tiring his arms. Normally, there wouldn't be any question he could make even a shot like this, but he's so out of practice.

But so am I. I couldn't do any better.

Father Ben has his eyes closed, quietly running his rosary beads through his fingers.

I trace the trail sign for 'Saint Des' on the console ledge in front of Josh. He nods. We sit and tap our fingertips together silently to keep track together as we recite the chaplet in our heads, our eyes never leaving the landscape in front of us. Harry joins in too, on my other side, though he's clearly distracted because his taps don't always happen.

Please, Lord. If we could even just find out for certain what happened. I mean, justice would be really good, too.

But even just to know for sure…

Finally…the faint sound of an engine wafts through the open windows. Maurice's silver truck comes into sight. It's the one that used to be his road truck, but battered enough that it's clearly been downgraded to be his farm runaround for some time.

We let it pass. He pulls up to the gate and waits a few moments, clearly looking around nearby for predators since it's only a single gate. Finally, the gate opens. In he drives. Gate closed. He drives around the inside of the fence, inspecting it, then stops outside the door to the house. In he goes.

Again, we wait. And wait. And…

The door's opening. Josh stiffens, Harry goes rigid. Father Ben sits tensely.

I check my watch. Forty-three minutes. About average. No sign of a worker with Mau, though the guy will probably use his own vehicle. Mau closes the door and gets into the truck. Soon he's through the gate and driving back down the valley. As soon as he's out of sight of the house…

Smoothly, silently, Josh rises from his seat and settles on the sniping boards, raising his rifle into position. I lean my head close to him, my eyes no longer on Mau but on the wind gauge. "North-north-west, nine-eighty, six," I read softly. "North-north-west, nine-eighty, six-six. North-north-west, nine-seventy, six-eight…" Clearly, steadily, I keep reading, so he always has the most up-to-date possible wind info without having to move his eyes from his sights.

Out of the corner of my eye, I can see Father Ben's fingers gripping his rosary, knuckles showing white against his dark skin.

Josh slowly breathes out, his finger starting to tighten…

Thud. The whole 'Vi lurches as something strikes hard against our side.

Josh inhales sharply, his finger flying off the trigger, head lifting away from his sights.

One glance and he hisses, *"Outage!"*

A bull steg — our friend from yesterday? — has just rammed us hard with its shoulder. Only the confined space we're parked in is preventing it from swinging its thagomizer. Thank God, because there's no way Maurice wouldn't hear *that* hitting us!

Bellowing, the bull rams into us again.

We only have one completely silent shot and Mau will soon be out of range…

Josh is already going completely flat once more, jerking his chin sharply at me before putting his eye to the sights.

"North-north-west, nine-sixty, six-seven," I say — *thud, lurch!* "North-north-west, nine-eighty, six-six…" *Thud, lurch!*

Curse that stupid creature! How can Josh possibly… I tap Harry sharply on the knee, pointing at the steg without looking, but don't stop reading the wind to Josh.

Harry gets it. "Clear…clear…impact in three, two, one, now"—*thud, lurch!*—"clear now, clear, clear, coming again, three, two…"

Josh squeezes the trigger. The shot is quietly audible in the turret, but won't carry far.

Thud. The steg shoulders us again a second later.

Mau's so far away, now, Josh didn't fire a moment too soon. For a moment I think he missed…then the truck veers sharply to the left, the flat tire dragging through the grass. Maurice brings it safely to a halt, but through our sights we can see him thump the steering wheel in frustration.

"So," murmurs Father Ben. "Will he call for help?"

"Let's move." Josh slides down the ladder.

If Mau's visits to this place are innocent, he'll soon have someone out here to provide cover while he puts his spare wheel on. We need to get there first.

If the place isn't innocent, we need to get there before he's taken a good enough look around to risk jumping out—and realized that his tire didn't burst from natural causes.

We're far enough away now that, with the wind as it is, there's no risk of him hearing our engine as Josh starts it up.

"Get out the way, you deranged creature," mutters Josh, engaging in a shoving match with the bull as it tries to keep us trapped. "All right, how about this?" He flicks several switches, turning on every front-facing light the 'Vi has, including some eye-piercingly bright floodlights.

The steg reels back, making a warbling sound of fright—then turns tail and runs.

"Finally," mutters Josh, flicking the lights off again and easing us free of the crags.

Down around the back at high speed, through a slight gap between hillocks, and there's the silver truck ahead of us. No sign of any vehicle approaching to help, yet.

We're so well cammed up, Mau will never recognize this 'Vi, which he only saw once, two years ago. Josh has put on the black wig, letting the hair hang around his face. Invisible behind the nets, I help Harry and Father Ben check the area for danger as we approach.

In moments, we're rolling to a halt beside Mau's truck. "It's all clear," I tell Josh over the intercom, then I slide quickly down the ladder, followed by Harry and Father Ben. We all slip behind the partial rear pen partition that's been put in place specially.

"Hey, silver truck, you need a hand?" From the cab, we can hear Josh speaking over the interCar, making his voice even deeper than it's gotten recently. "We can cover you, if you like."

Silence from Mau for a few moments. Thinking?

"That'd be helpful." Really? He's not just saying *someone's coming already, clear off my land?* "What are you guys out hunting?" Forced politeness in Mau's voice. He really does want our help.

"Ain't hunting nothing here," says Josh. "Heading to Kennick Hills from Wiskcoming Flats. Yeah, we're too lazy to take the camo down and put it straight up again, sue us."

"Well, it's your own nets you're wearing out," says Mau, in a genial tone.

"Sure are. Well, I bet you know that Utahraptors often gather back only a little ways, so we'd better do a proper check 'fore you get going on that tire. You may as well jump aboard and have a cuppa Jo rather'n sit in there and freeze y'self. Turret, he clear to come over? Yeh, turret confirms all clear," Josh carefully doesn't give Mau a chance to excuse himself. "Opening the side door now."

We crowd around to peep through the feeding slot in the partition. Refusing to come over would be suspicious, if Mau does have anything to hide—and unlikely behavior, if he don't. So it's no surprise at all when a familiar stocky figure, rifle over shoulder, clambers up through the door—which slides closed behind him. And locks.

My heart starts to hammer in my chest.

We have him.

HARRY

The cab door hisses open and Josh appears, his rifle trained on Uncle Mau.

"Don't move. Not one muscle."

Uncle Mau goes motionless. Josh has pulled off the wig, leaving his prison stubble bare.

"*Joshua?* I thought you were in jail."

"I'm fresh from nine months inside—which I reckon you bear some responsibility for. So don't try nothing, got that?"

Uncle Mau stands rigid, but speaks in a deliberately calming tone—though an edge of anger peeks through. "Look, Joshua, I don't understand what bone you think you've got to pick with me. I did my best to prevent them finding you all…" He trails off as Darryl steps out, me behind her. We both keep our guns on him. Father Ben follows us.

Uncle Mau stands with his lips slightly apart, saying nothing. The blood drains from his face, leaving it a sickly grayish color.

"Hey, kids." He finally speaks. "What…whatever are you all doing out here?" His attempt at a casual tone falls flatter than roadkill.

"Father Ben, you're up," says Josh, nodding toward Uncle Mau.

Father Ben steps forward and takes the rifle from Maurice's shoulder, leaning it out of the way against a cupboard, then quickly patting Mau down. He relieves him of a belt knife, a penknife, and several fence fobs, then he steps back again.

"What...what are you all *doing* here?" asks Uncle Mau, still attempting to sound puzzled, but rather short on the level of blustering anger I would expect from him. "Why are you threatening me?"

Father Ben checks through the windows, then shakes his head. Still no one approaching to help. That's interesting. Shouldn't the worker from the house be here by now? Darryl exchanges a glance with Josh, who gives a slight nod. I want to speak, to challenge Uncle Mau—*Maurice*—but I can't think of anything to say.

"Why don't we head back to that little house of yours and have a chat?" says Darryl.

"We can chat right here," says Maurice, too quickly. "Or, uh, head back to the farmhouse? Much more comfortable."

"No," says Josh. "I think we'll take a look around your little place up there. Or is there some problem with that?"

"There's...nothing of interest there. Let's go to the farmhouse."

Josh jerks his head to the cab. "Harry, if you please."

I walk wide around Maurice, behind the others— lines of fire, lines of fire, lines of fire!—slip into the cab and settle into the driver's seat. Father Ben's now pointing Mau's rifle at him, but he's made it clear he doesn't feel a priest should actually shoot anyone, so it's just for show. But Josh and Darryl have their guns trained on the swine, which should be enough.

I start the engine and pull away very, very carefully, avoiding any sudden jolts that might allow Maurice to try something. I go super slow, and when we reach the house, I pull to a halt equally gently while Father Ben activates the fob. Then we're inside, and the gate is closed. I head back into the living area.

Maurice stands with his back to the wall. Despite the cold day, sweat coats his pale forehead, emphasizing the way his hair is receding. His eyes are wide, and he's breathing too fast. He looks like a cornered animal.

"Okay, Maurice," says Josh. "Let's go take a look in that house."

"You…" Maurice moistens his lips as though they're bone dry. "You have to listen to me. Let me explain…"

"*Explain?*" I demand, anger finally unlocking my tongue. "What? Why you killed our dad?"

"I didn't! I *swear*! But you *have* to listen to me before you hear a load of…of totally mixed-up nonsense…"

"*Hear?* What do you mean?" I'm yelling, but I barely notice. "Hear from *who*?" I hit the door button and leap out. I nearly sprint right over to the house, then remember I'm supposed to be helping guard

Mau—who looks desperate enough to try anything.

With great effort, I force myself to stand and cover Maurice as Josh and Darryl shepherd him down from the 'Vi and climb down one by one after him. Josh made a big point about us not getting too close to Maurice, so I even back up a bit. I force myself to keep thinking about our lines of fire, the other thing Josh drilled into us over and over again. A rifle bullet will go through more than one person, at this range especially, and all that.

Finally, everyone is out, and we're at the door. And then we're inside. In a hallway. There's a staircase, going up to the other level, but the whole of the ground floor is sealed off by a very solid metal door secured with a number pad. A very new looking metal door.

"Listen, *please*." Uncle Mau's *begging*, his hands clenched together. "Darryl, Harry, *please listen to me…*"

Darryl's face has gone as white as Mau's, as she stares at that door.

"Open it." When Mau doesn't move, she rams her rifle tip right into his chest, hard enough to hurt. "*Open it!*"

Finally, Mau reaches for the keypad. Types in some numbers.

"*Darryl?*" A voice comes from behind the door. A voice I haven't heard for two years. It comes again, quick and frantic. "Maurice? Don't you hurt my kids! Don't you *dare* hurt my kids!"

I stare at the door, the skin of my face fuzzing strangely. Have I gone as white as Darryl?

"Dad?"

JOSHUA

Darryl and Harry, I can tell outta the corner of my eye, are staring at the door, no attention for Maurice at all. Even Father Ben is shooting it a wide-eyed look. Maurice's eyes shift; he tenses…

I cock my rifle in a superfluous, but nicely attention-grabbing, way. "Oh no," I murmur. "You ain't *my* uncle anything. *Don't.*"

Maurice's shoulders slump. *"You've got to listen,"* he whispers, but Darryl's already pulling the heavy door open.

"Don't you hurt them, Maurice!" shouts that voice.

"I think you underestimate your kids, Will," Maurice says tiredly, as a sturdy—though less stocky than Maurice—guy appears behind the opening door. He's about Wilhelm's age with brown hair slightly graying at the temples and a significant beer gut. The man surges forward, then stands, staring and blinking in surprise at the scene before him.

"Darryl? Harry?"

Safety catches hastily applied, they throw themselves on him. Maurice eyes me dully and makes no move this time. Not a slow learner.

William Franklyn has staggered back under Darryl and Harry's onslaught, and Father Ben steps into the room after them, still staring in astonishment, though a grin is starting to spread over his face. Then he moves where I can't see him without taking my eyes from Maurice. I don't like being stuck out here in the hall with the villain. Too easy for him to try to dart away and get back outside—or simply jump me.

"Go on," I tilt my head fractionally toward the doorway.

Maurice takes a deep breath, like he's getting more scared by the moment. "All right," he says in a low voice. "But you've got to give me a hearing. And for pity's sake, don't give Will a gun!"

Afraid Darryl and Harry's dad will take justice into his own hands? Well, if you keep someone imprisoned in your dank dungeon for almost two years, you can expect them to be super pissed off!

Maurice finally steps into the room, putting his back to the wall I wave him toward, where there's no possibility of anyone getting behind him and blocking my line of fire. Father Ben remembers that we have a prisoner and points Maurice's rifle again, so I manage to sneak a few lightning-fast glances around the room.

My brows scrunch together in puzzlement.

It *ain't* no dank dungeon. We've entered a large living room furnished with comfy sofas and armchairs, expensive multimedia screen, a desk and chair, even an exercise corner with a shiny treadmill, weights, and pull-up bars. Framed photos of Darryl and Harry and their mom and others of a glamorous-looking woman hang on one wall. Several empty beer bottles and a variety of potato chips and candy packets lie on the table in front of the seating area, along with a stack of dirty plates.

From the look of it, Maurice has gone to considerable effort to make his captive as comfortable—and at home—as possible.

This just keeps getting weirder and weirder.

DARRYL

"Darryl, Harry, ah, kids!" Dad's no sooner released us than he pulls us straight back in for another hug. "It's so good to see you!"

I cling on tightly, equally reluctant to let him go. Joy fills me so full I can barely draw in a breath.

"Dad, you're alive," I whisper, tears starting to leak from my eyes, though I know it's not very Hunterly of me to cry while we've still got a dangerous prisoner to deal with.

Oh yeah, oops… I throw a glance over my shoulder, but Josh and Father Ben have Maurice under close guard. Beside me, Harry is sobbing un-restrainedly into Dad's other shoulder.

"Dad, we thought you were *dead*," I sniff.

"Much he cared." I only just catch the bitter mutter from Maurice, but it makes me pull away from Dad at last and shoot him a glare, which draws Dad's attention to him as well.

"Maurice, you scum," snaps Dad. "Boot's on the other foot now, huh?"

Although he keeps his rifle trained on Maurice, a faint frown wrinkles Josh's brow, like something is puzzling him. I glance around the room, almost afraid to look, but it's…comfortable. Luxurious, even. And downright homey. Those photos on the wall are from our living room at home, I recognize the frames. Maurice must have brought them here. And those ornaments on the shelf. Everywhere I look, I see things I recognize.

If Maurice hates Dad enough to imprison him like this, why keep him so comfortably, go to all that effort? Come to that, why is Dad even alive? I sure ain't complaining, but no wonder Josh looks perplexed.

"Dad, what in Saint Des's name has been going on?" I ask, as Harry finally detaches from Dad, wiping his face on his sleeve and grinning through his ragged breathing.

"This treacherous back-stabber is out to get me, that's what!"

"But…you're *alive*," says Harry, puzzlement spreading over his face as the oddness of the situation begins to strike him too.

"Only because he's too cowardly to actually do the deed."

But that doesn't make sense. Surely if Maurice wanted Dad dead, he'd keep him in bad conditions and hope he got weak and died in a way that would make him feel less directly responsible?

"Will somebody *please* listen to me?" Maurice's voice is stronger, more demanding. He's recovering from the shock. "Will is not himself. He's confused…"

"*Confused?*" Dad snarls. "I'll give you confused, you treacherous—"

I catch his arm quickly as he surges forward. "Dad, Dad, never mind him for now. There's…there's something…I need to make sure you know. Let's…let's sit down."

Wonderful as this reunion is, I can't bear to let it go another moment without making sure he…*knows.*

Dad sinks down into the sofa. Harry plops beside him. I take an armchair. Josh and Father Ben remain standing, covering Maurice.

"What is it?" Dad asks.

"It's…it's Carol…"

Anguish sweeps across his face—yeah, he already knows—closely followed by fury of an intensity I've never seen there before. "Yeah, the murdering— I'll settle him right now!" He grabs at my rifle, and I barely realize his intention in time to swing it out of the way.

"Hey, Dad," I say lightly, trying to calm the

situation. Surely he isn't really gonna...? "That's rude."

"Rude?"

"Hunter rules," says Father Ben. "No touching other people's guns. I believe."

"Darryl, you're not a hunter," snaps Dad, his eyes on Maurice. "Now give me your gun so I can deal with this murdering son of a—" Dad lunges.

I evade him by popping up out of the armchair and taking a few steps away. Hampered by a considerable beer gut that he didn't have before, Dad flounders up more slowly.

I step sideways. "Come on, Dad, we can't just shoot him! He belongs in jail."

Father Ben's frowning. Harry eyes Dad uneasily. Josh stands impassively, most of his attention on Maurice, though he's clearly listening hard, and I'm not sure what he'd do if Dad actually got hold of a gun.

Dad stands for a moment, draws a couple of deep breaths, clearly trying to let his anger go. "Yeah. Yeah," he mutters at last. "He belongs in jail. Yeah. *No*," he shakes his head, the anguish leaking back into his eyes. "Too good for him, jail! After what he did to Carol..."

Harry shoots me a wide-eyed look.

"Dad," I say. "Maurice didn't do anything to Carol."

Dad snorts. "Sure, not with his own two hands! But it's his fault she's...that she's—" He breaks off as though his throat is too tight to get the words out.

"How is it his fault?" I ask warily.

Dad stares at me incredulously. "*How?* Because he kidnapped me, and she was scared on the farm alone and tried to drive to the city and— You know the rest, you were there, weren't you? Or did he lie about that, too?" He glowers at Maurice, his fingers flexing as though he'd still love to wrap them around a rifle butt—or maybe the stocky man's neck.

I stare at him, my stomach like an elevator that's had its cables cut. "*Maurice* kidnapped you?"

"Of course. You must know that; you're here, aren't you?" Dad seems astonished by the question. He eyes Maurice, his expression vicious. "Yeah. Yeah, even if they can't charge him over Carol…they'll put him away for the kidnapping. For a long, long time. You're finally going to get what's coming to you, Maurice."

Harry shoots me another look, his eyes wide with horror. Father Ben's lips are parted in dismay, only half his attention on Maurice. Josh is frowning harder than ever, though his gaze don't shift. I stare at Dad, speechless. I'm starting to have a really, really bad feeling about what's been going on here.

The silence stretches on. And on.

"Why are you all looking at me like that?" complains Dad, dropping back onto the sofa, puffing slightly as though he hasn't been using all that shiny new exercise equipment in the corner at all.

I moisten my lips, my stomach flipping along with my heart in dull heavy thuds. "Dad…Maurice isn't the one who kidnapped you."

Dad snorts. "Oh, he's already filled your ears with his lies, has he? That nonsense about how he bought me from two hunters to save my life? Well, you can ignore that. He's just trying to save his own skin."

I look properly at Maurice for the first time since we entered the room. He stands tensely, despair slumping his shoulders, but there's an edge of anger in his defiant eyes.

O Lord, help us. This is…

"*Now* why are you looking at me like that?" grumbles Dad.

"Because…" I swallow. "Because…Maurice didn't tell us nothing, Dad. We already knew when we came here who kidnapped you and on whose orders. We came here precisely because we knew that Maurice had bought you from the kidnappers. To kill you, he told them, but clearly that wasn't true."

Maurice's eyes widen. His lips part, but it seems to be a moment before he can speak, his chest heaving. The hope that floods his face is…painful…to watch. "You know?" he splutters at last. "You know the truth?"

"That much of it," I say cautiously. "I don't know why, if you claim you bought Dad to save his life, he's still locked up in *here*."

"You *can't* listen to him!" explodes Dad. "He's lying filth! He as good as killed Carol, and he was going to kill me eventually, when he worked up the nerve! He wants my good pasture, my whole farm! I'll see him in jail if it's the last thing I do, *I swear to God I will!*" his voice rises hysterically.

Maurice regards Dad with grim resignation, then looks at me. "*That* is why he's still locked up in here. I've got four kids who've already lost their mom. I'm not letting them lose their dad too, not if I can help it. I'm sorry it meant you and Harry thinking he was dead—but you went off with Joshua and were happy enough, as Father Ben told it. My own kids had to come first." He lets out a long breath and adds, his voice shaking slightly, "But I am really, really sorry, you two, especially about this last year. I'd have got you back out of the city if I possibly could."

"How could you keep Dad locked up like this if you really care?" Harry protests.

"What else was I supposed to do?" Maurice's voice firms again. "I bought him from two hunters whose identities I don't know in a top secret transaction in the middle of nowhere. All the evidence would prove that he's been here in this house since then. If he claimed I was the one who kidnapped him, how can I prove otherwise?" His eyes brighten. "But...how did you know? Is there evidence?"

"The word of a dead man," I say.

Maurice's face falls. Dad slaps a hand down on the coffee table, hard, toppling an empty beer bottle. "*Enough!* Darryl, this is nonsense! *Maurice* kidnapped me!"

"No. He didn't." I draw a deep breath. "Look… let's all sit down and go through this. All of us." I jerk my head at Mau and Josh.

Ignoring Dad's protests, Josh points Mau to the desk chair, which is furthest from Dad (and the door) and allows him to maintain a clear line of fire. Even if Maurice may not be quite as much the villain of the piece as we thought, he's not only a cornered animal, but also, by his own admission, a mother animal defending her cubs—the two most dangerous things combined. Josh ain't gonna let his guard down yet.

Father Ben settles on the sofa on Dad's other side and grips his arm for a moment. "I'm so glad to see you alive and well, William. But I think you need to listen to what everyone has to say. There does seem to have been a terrible misunderstanding."

The words of a respected grown-up like Father Ben finally make Dad fall silent, though he goes on glowering sullenly at Mau.

"Maurice?" I say, when it's clear Josh means to remain standing. "Why don't you go first? Tell us your side of things."

Maurice nods. "Well, there's not much to tell. I

thought Will was dead, same as we all did, after finding the breach. Then some skinny hunter came up to me in the pastures later that day. His 'Vi was parked almost out of sight, only the turret showing, though I guess he had cover. Started a shifty conversation about William and"—Maurice flushes, shame lowering his eyes—"about William and...and some stupid things I'd said while drunk in-city."

Maurice shakes his head. "Didn't take me long to figure out that he was asking me, very discreetly, if I'd meant what I said. Well, I hadn't, of course. I'm a mean drunk, I'll freely admit it. S'why I don't ever drink too much at home. Only in-city now and then, on a supply run. But something about this guy...well, it put me on alert, right from the start."

Josh smiles wryly, like he understands this statement completely.

"So," Maurice continues, "I didn't rush to disavow what I'd said, and thank God I didn't—though it'd sure have saved me some trouble if I had," he adds sourly. "Anyway, turned out they had Will, and it didn't take me that long to figure out that they were only going to hand him over to me if they were convinced I had it in for him. So I played along, said what the snake wanted to hear. Eventually the guy seemed satisfied. So we arranged to meet again later that afternoon, once I'd sorted out the money they wanted, and that's what we did. I was out getting Will from them when you called, Darryl, right before you left with Carol."

I swallow. "Bentley told me you'd gone to see a man about something."

"Yeah, well, that something was your dad. He was thoroughly tranked when they handed him over, so I drove him to this old place and heaved him inside and settled him down to sleep it off."

"Why didn't you just bring him straight home?" demands Harry.

"I was scared," says Mau bluntly.

"About the tranquilizers?" I ask. "But they're super-safe nowadays."

"With the right dose, they are," Mau agrees. "Not knowing if the hunters had a clue what they were doing—or cared, considering their original task—I was a little nervous whether he'd wake up okay, yeah. I figured there was no point risking trouble with the hunters if he simply died. Everyone thought he was dead already—far less risk of the hunters coming after me if I just left it that way. And that was the other thing I was worried about. I'd just sworn blind to that shifty guy that I was going to kill Will. What would they do when Will popped back up alive? Would they do anything? How were we going to handle it? I wanted to talk to Will, figure out a plan, before simply making it public knowledge he was alive."

"But we thought he was *dead!*" objects Harry.

"And you let us!"

Mau nods. "Yeah, but how many people in both our families could have gotten hurt if the hunters came after us? I went along to your farm the next morning and I kept my mouth shut, I admit. Because I didn't know he was going to wake up. And if he didn't, why upset you all over again by giving you false hope? I figured I'd come back here afterwards and, all being well, he'd be awake; we could chew the problem over and in an hour or two I could bring him home and make you all very happy. Instead, I arrived that morning and found out what had happened to Carol. So when I got here and Will was awake and wondering why he was locked up in my old worker house, instead of telling him what happened and us having a good laugh about how I'd tricked that evil hunter, I had to tell him that—" Mau breaks off, swallowing, eyes haunted.

"Well, to say he didn't take it well would be the biggest understatement I ever made," he goes on eventually. "I could not convince him then, nor at any time since, that I wasn't responsible for it all. I guess it's the grief. He isn't thinking clearly. He's not himself, really. He won't do anything, he just sits around and— Heck, I come in here most days and talk to him, try to, try to—" Mau makes uncharacteristically helpless flapping gestures with his hands. "Well, it doesn't do any good. He hates me, as you can see. Swears he'll see me in jail the instant I set him free—or he manages to escape. I put that metal door in because I wasn't prepared to risk that, I admit." He jabs a finger toward the hall. "But I *didn't* kidnap him, and if he'd only have promised not to put me in jail, I would have released him."

"Nonsense," mutters Dad, who's been huffing indignantly throughout Mau's narration. "Total nonsense!"

But it's not. In fact, it rings completely true. Maurice saved Dad. Probably forked out a heck of a lot of money to do it, too.

And Dad's been making his life miserable ever since.

HARRY

Darryl looks slightly green around the face and I know how she feels. Everything's making me feel quite literally sick. Dad could have come back to us any time, if he'd just been prepared to believe what his best friend was telling him? I don't want to accept it, but it's the truth.

"Why are you even taking this nonsense seriously?" grumbles Dad.

"I'm sorry, Dad." Darryl speaks very evenly. "It's the truth. Josh had it from the lips of one of the hunters who sold you to Mau."

"Then Mau hired them in the first place!"

"No." Darryl swallows, then speaks very firmly. "They were hired by Martin Selman."

Dad's eyes widen, his lips parting like he's just been punched in the gut. "You're lying!"

Darryl flinches, face tightening in pain. "I'm not—"

Dad waves a hand, back-tracking. "Not *you*, I didn't mean— But someone's lying!"

"You jumped to a false conclusion, Dad." Darryl speaks in a very soft, reasonable tone. "It was an easy mistake to make." She shoots an apologetic glance at Mau for these tactical words, since Dad's still staring into space. "But it *was* a mistake. Mau bought you to save your life, and the only reason he won't let you go is because he thinks you'll put him in jail and ruin him and his children's lives."

"It's true, Dad," I whisper, since he still looks downright mulish. "It was Carol's brother. She obviously never told him about the will. You remember she said he was hard up for money right then? That's why she was going to let him stay in her apartment."

"He's a realtor," says Father Ben, "so he knew what the farm was worth. Probably thought at the very least he'd get to sell it for her, and that most likely she'd be generous with her unexpected windfall. Unless he was a *total* monster and meant to do away with her too, but that's less likely."

Dad stares dully at the table for a while longer, his lips twitching now and then like he's about to speak. "Then…" he whispers hoarsely, at long last.

"Maurice saved your life," Darryl repeats. "And it's probably about time you thanked him."

JOSHUA

My heart aches for Darryl and Harry, who've both been looking downright queasy at this painful turn of events. I'm feeling unexpectedly sorry for our prisoner, too, though I don't take my rifle from him yet. Until he's convinced we ain't a threat to him and his family, we can't be sure he ain't a threat to us.

Just exactly what are we gonna *do* about this? It ain't simple, that's for sure.

Obviously William Franklyn can't remain imprisoned. And he may be physically fine, but he's obviously not well. I hope Darryl and Harry can see that, though I reckon they can. From the anxious wrinkle in Father Ben's brow as he watches his long-lost parishioner, he sees it clearly.

But Maurice Carr don't belong in jail. Sure, strictly speaking he shouldn't really have kept Mr. Franklyn locked up, no matter what Mr. Franklyn threatened, but it sure is hard to blame him, under the circumstances. If kidnapping can get you twenty-five years, illegal imprisonment will surely get you something similar. How can we let that happen?

But how can we save *both* of 'em? William Franklyn's been officially dead for the better part of two years. The authorities are gonna need a good explanation for his sudden reanimation. How do we provide one that won't see Maurice straight behind bars?

From the way the hope on Maurice's face has faded back into sick apprehension, he sees the problem too.

No, I ain't taking my gun off him just yet.

HARRY

"So," says Father Ben in a very calm voice, "we need to think what we're going to do about all this."

Do? We're going home with Dad, surely!

"Martin Selman belongs in jail!" says Dad fiercely. "And those hunters, too!"

"One of the hunters is dead," says Father Ben. "And there isn't enough proof to do anything about Selman or the other one. No, we need to decide what to do about this situation right here. You and Maurice."

"Yes," says Darryl slowly. "How do you come back to life without it incriminating Mau?"

Oh. I hadn't thought about that, yet. Awkward. I'm still mad at Uncle Mau for keeping Dad all this time, but I guess he doesn't actually deserve prison. I mean, he did save Dad's life…

"Mr. Franklyn doesn't actually know who kidnapped him," says Josh, speaking for the first time. "So he could answer a whole loada police questions with variations of 'I don't know who kidnapped me' and 'I never saw their faces' without telling a single lie."

"But if they ask him how he got rescued," says Darryl. "Right now he can say he never saw where he was being held because he was brought in unconscious. But the moment he walks outside…"

Josh has a very thoughtful expression on his face. "The most important question," he says, "is this. If it can be arranged that he could answer those awkward questions both without lying *and* without incriminating Maurice, would he wish to?"

"Would you, Dad?" asks Darryl?

"Would you protect your best friend?" asks Father Ben.

"Who saved your life," I add for good measure, since I have the feeling from the way Darryl and Josh are watching Dad that how Dad responds is very important, though I'm not sure precisely why.

Dad stares at the table for a while. Eventually, he shoots a look at Uncle Mau, not quite meeting his eyes. "He really didn't…?"

"He really didn't," says Darryl, *very* firmly.

"Then, yeah," mutters Dad. "I'd protect him if I could."

"Good," says Josh. "We'd better think how to do it, then." Finally taking his attention from Mau for longer than a split second, he stares steadily at Darryl. She stares back, and it's one of those annoying moments where I just know they each know what the other is thinking and I don't.

"Yeah," says Darryl. "We'd better think about it." She gives the tiniest nod.

What?

Josh jerks his rifle slightly. "Maurice, you come out here with me and let 'em talk."

Looking startled, eyes narrowed in wariness, Maurice allows Josh to shepherd him from the room.

"Where are they going?" I demand.

"Dad ain't the only one who needs to be able to answer questions honestly with *I don't know, I don't know* and *I don't know,*" says Darryl. "Well, I guess Mau might not care so much about that, but we should."

Maurice being quite a fierce atheist, and of a somewhat, what's the expression?—utilitarian?— mindset, I guess she's right about that.

"But don't we need Josh's help figuring this out?"

"I'm sure we'll cope."

Huh. Yeah, she and Josh have figured it out already, haven't they? Without saying a word to each other. They just haven't filled the rest of us in, yet.

Being around two people who are on the same wavelength to that degree can be annoying sometimes.

"Is that the hunter boy you two ran off with?" asks Dad, looking after Josh with a frown, like he's only just really noticed him.

"That's Josh, yes," says Darryl.

"I don't know what he was thinking, taking you out there like that."

"Come on, Dad," says Darryl. "I was only a little younger than you were when you and Mau ran off and worked in a 'Vi for a season."

"Several *years* younger!" says Dad. "And Harry was *much* younger. Anyway, that was completely different!"

"Oh?" Darryl's voice goes sharp. "I suppose it was. We needed a home and a job if we were gonna stay out-city and try to save you—you and Mau just did it for kicks."

Yikes! That went downhill fast.

"So, uh, what are we going to do?" I say brightly, as Father Ben winces and Dad frowns.

Darryl lets out a breath and manages to smile. "Uh, well, Dad, you just need to remember that whatever they ask you, you say some variation of 'I don't know who kidnapped me' and 'I never saw the place I was held' and 'I don't know how I came to be free,' okay?"

"The last one's a lie," I can't help saying, shooting a look at Father Ben.

"I'm sure it will work out," says Darryl airily.

"I'm not," says Dad sourly. "How can I say that? I know exactly who rescued me and how I came to be free. And I'm gonna see the outside of here in a moment and then—" He breaks off with a slight grunt. A blank look spreads over his face—then he slumps back on the sofa, head lolling—and begins to breathe deeply and evenly.

"Woah!" Father Ben plucks a tranquilizer dart from Dad's arm—the one closest to the door.

Only then do I realize what just happened.

I look at the doorway—the tip of a tranquilizer gun peeping around the frame is all I can see. Even if Dad had looked that way at the wrong moment, he wouldn't have been able to recognize Josh, hidden in the shadows of the hall behind the gun sights.

"*Short-circuiting fences*," I exclaim. "You and Josh don't mess around, Darryl!"

"Ain't no other way," says Josh, walking into the room now he's sure Dad's completely out.

"Where's Maurice?" asks Father Ben, eyeing Dad's slumped form with disquiet but not bothering to object now the deed is done.

"In the 'Vi. The systems are all locked and I have the keys; he can't do nothing nor go nowhere. And if we put him back in his truck and send him home before we bring your dad outta here, he can say truthfully that he don't know how your dad got dumped in front of your gates just before he arrived there today."

And Dad can say truthfully that he doesn't know how this happened. Ruthless—but effective.

I just really hope Josh got the dosage right.

I wouldn't even bother wondering, if it wasn't Dad.

But it is.

DARRYL

Harry keeps watch while Josh and Father Ben heave Dad out of the 'Vi and lay him on the roadway, half-way between the inner and outer fences and safely beyond the eye of the Franklyn farm's gatecam. I follow, holding the nice little note we've prepared in my gloved hand. We cut the letters out of a sealed magazine from a pile Mau had clearly provided for Dad, never previously opened, to avoid any chance of DNA contamination.

Harry insisted on doing the actual cutting and sticking—gloved, and with a scarf tied over his mouth to avoid saliva droplets settling on anything—on the grounds that he's under-eighteen and would get the lightest punishment if the authorities were to figure out we prepared the note and try to pin the original kidnapping on us. By the time he'd done it, Mau had finished changing his tire and driven off, and we were able to go back to the little house to retrieve Dad and Father Ben.

The note is our one chance to point the police in the right direction, so we agreed unanimously that we're gonna take the—very slight—risk.

I read it one last time as Josh carefully arranges Dad in the recovery position so he'll be safe to be left for a few minutes until Mau arrives.

MARTIN SELMAN,
YOU DIDN'T PAY US ENOUGH
TO KEEP HIM FOR THIS LONG
SO YOU CAN HAVE HIM BACK.

Short and sweet. And not even a lie. Who knows whether the police can do anything, on such scant evidence? But at least it'll put Selman on their radar.

I fold the note and bend to fasten it to Dad's collar with a safety pin.

"I'll see you soon, Dad," I murmur, though he can't hear me.

And when I do, he'll be officially alive again. That's gonna change everything.

"Let's move," says Josh.

We shift the 'Vi a good distance away and park behind a field shelter that screens all but the turret from view, then watch over Dad's distant, unconscious form, rifles in hand. We really don't wanna have to start shooting, though, unless we absolutely have to. They're bound to question Mau about whether he saw or heard anything suspicious around the time that he found Dad—the less there is to tell, the less likely we'll end up in the police's sights—or that Mau will end up telling a parcel of lies that might come back to bite him, quite apart from the obvious objection.

We don't have long to wait. Right on time, Mau's new road truck—shiny and white—comes into view in the distance, soon screeching to a halt in front of the body on the ground—Mau knew he needed to be on time, but not why, though he may have guessed. He jumps out after only the briefest of pauses to check for danger and hurries over to Dad.

After taking a few quick pictures of the scene with his ScreamerBand, he's soon dragging Dad toward his truck and painstakingly heaving him up into it. Through our gun sights we can see him wiping sweat from his brow—Dad's not exactly a lightweight, to move around—then leaning over the center of the dashboard. Josh taps a few controls on the console and manages to tune into the WhatHap signal so we can listen.

"This is Highway Patrol, what is your emergency?"

"I have an unconscious man. I'll head for Exception City on route M-four-three-nine, can you send an ambulance? And the police. I've reason to believe this may be a kidnapping victim."

"Understood. Proceed on route M-four-three-nine and you will be met along the way. Police will also attend your current location. Confirm that it is the scene of the crime?"

"It's where he's been dumped, yes. I'll toss down a shovel so they can find the spot. I took pictures."

"Understood. Highway Patrol out."

The white truck pulls away at speed. No way we'll be able to keep up.

Father Ben climbs down from the turret and Josh prepares to follow, keen to get underway so we're well gone before the police arrive to look for clues.

"Josh!" Harry sounds tense. "Three o'clock, six hundred feet."

I shoot a glance that way. A steg bull—oh, not the same one, surely?—is ambling determinedly in our direction, tiny head turning this way and that, lethal spiked tail swinging gently behind it. Oh no. Seriously?

"Josh?" says Harry again, pointing his rifle uncertainly at the approaching critter. But Maurice is still close enough to hear the shot…

Josh slides down the ladder and dives into the cab, saying over his shoulder, "We'll try to drive away."

The bull walks straight past a tasty shrub that's sprouted near the field shelter, still heading our way. Far more interested in locating females at this time of year than in food. Or rival males?

I mean, what's it doing here in this farmed pasture? No females here. It's not following us, is it, the single-minded beast?

The engine roars into life. I clutch the hatch guard rail as we lurch forward at full acceleration.

The steg's small head lifts, nostrils flaring. With shocking speed, it swings its thagomizer.

Smack.

The spikes lodge in the 'Vi's armor, the steg's weight making the wheels spin in the damp grass and halting our getaway. Harry winces. My heart jumps into my throat, pounding there. If it gets one of those huge spikes through the wheelguards and into a tire… We'll still be changing the wheel when the police arrive!

Quickly, I track the target with my rifle, my finger tightening on the trigger as the 'Vi lurches erratically forward, dragging the steg…

The steg yanks hard, trying to get its tail free, and the 'Vi jerks violently, tilting at a frightening angle. I get my finger off the trigger just in time, catching the console to stay up as Harry stumbles into me.

Yank. The 'Vi starts to tilt again, but I have my balance. Except… Argh! The steg's head is now too close to the side of the 'Vi for me to get the crosshairs onto its tiny brain. The back plates block a shot to its heart.

The engine roars as Josh engages diff lock for traction and turns sharply to the left. The yank on the trapped tail from a different angle drags the spikes free—snapping one clean off—and we're away again. This time our acceleration wins out, and we pull steadily ahead. By the time we pass under the outer fence onto the public road, we have a comfortable lead, so I'm surprised when Josh pulls to a halt, swinging the 'Vi around to the left so the driver's side faces the angry bull. At least, until, on the console screen, I see him lower the cab window and raise his rifle.

Crack.

The bull drops to the ground with a thud, the broken thagomizer slamming down behind it a moment later.

"Okay, that deals with that," I say, closing the turret windows and heading below.

When I enter the cab, Harry and Father Ben close behind, Josh is peering at the distant steg as though regretting that we won't have time to harvest the back plates, spikes, and hide. "Was that thing *following* us, Josh?"

"I reckon so. Better culled, anyway. Far too aggressive. Imagine if it picked on a smaller vehicle like Maurice's truck or an SOS van, let alone a little city-car."

Not a nice thought. Harry shivers and Father Ben winces. But there's no risk to anyone else, now.

We settle into our seats—except Perky who alternates springing from person to person seeking attention with running up and down the dashboard, clearly delighted to be out of the cage—and we're soon underway. We head off-road immediately since the police will probably question everyone in the area about what vehicles they saw around today.

As we drive, my mind goes back to Dad. Is everyone else as conscious as I am that we've put Dad totally at Mau's mercy?

If Mau wants to make absolutely sure Dad can't point the finger at him…

But no. He coulda done that any time. And he's called it in—he has to produce Dad, now, dead or alive. However he did it, forensics would probably figure it out.

"Why didn't we leave him out for the Wahlburgs to find when they arrive?" asks Harry suddenly, after we've been driving for a while. "Wouldn't that have been safer?"

"No, because we'd've had to leave him lying out there for Saint Des knows how long," says Josh, eyes front as he negotiates a shale slope. "No way to know exactly when they would arrive. And it's cold today, even leaving aside carni'saurs and him being tranked."

Yeah, Josh definitely thought about it too.

"Plus," says Father Ben, "if there's any chance your dad and Maurice's friendship can survive this, your dad needs to know once and for all that Maurice doesn't want to kill him. This will prove it, I hope, even to his satisfaction."

"Even?" says Harry, blankly. "What do you mean?"

"I simply mean," says Father Ben, "that your dad is paranoid at the moment. Not entirely without reason but…well, in other ways, as well, I think you may need to be patient with him for a while, okay?"

"Do you think we can get him some help?" I ask.

"If he'll accept it."

"He will have to *want* it," says Josh grimly.

"What kind of help?" asks Harry.

"From Mau's description," I say bluntly, "he's depressed, at the very least."

Harry's eyes widen in dismay. "Because of Carol?"

"You bet."

"I doubt being locked in that house for months on end, alone for most of every day, will have helped him pull through it, either," says Father Ben glumly. "Maurice sure was between a rock and a hard place, with that."

"If Dad were healthy, he woulda believed Mau," I say. "I don't have the slightest doubt about that."

"And I got the impression Maurice knows that," said Father Ben. "In fact, knowing Maurice's temper, it sounds like he's been exceptionally patient with your dad."

"Well, they've literally been friends since forever," I say, sighing. "And like you say, he obviously recognized that Dad's not well."

We drive in silence for a while. I have to try very hard to keep scanning the landscape rather than retreating into my own thoughts. I think Harry's watch-keeping is decidedly erratic as well. Father Ben does a little better, and Josh's eyes are never still.

I'm not really sure I *want* to think, right now.

Is Dad okay?

What will the authorities say?

And I just can't shut up that little voice that whispers: *Dad coulda come back to us, any time.*

Any time at all.

HARRY

Am I the only one who didn't stop to consider whether it was safe to let Mau take Dad in-city? Josh and Darryl clearly weighed the odds like good little hunters and concluded that it was safest overall. Father Ben wanted to give Mau the benefit of the doubt. And I didn't think about it.

I didn't realize how unwell Dad might be, either. I mean, I could tell something was off. He wasn't acting right. But if he's actually got 'depression.' That's scary. But it can be treated, right?

If he'll let them.

But surely just being free and going back to the farm and having life go back to normal will make a huge difference?

Without Carol, though. But his old normal, at least…

Normal. What is normal, now? In my head, normal always means the farm. But for months, what 'normal' actually brought to mind was life in the 'Vi. Now, normal…ugh, *now* normal brings thoughts of Susannah and Philip's clean white apartment! I really have been in-city too long.

No longer! In the next few days—even as soon as tomorrow?—surely Darryl and I will be in a car with Dad, on our way home? Finally!

I feel so happy right now I could almost forgive that Wilhelm guy!

Almost.

Oh thank you, Saint Des! Thanks, Lord!

DARRYL

Josh pulls up beside a bus stop on the main city ring road. "Harry, can you get to your foster-home from here?"

Harry peers at the numbers on the sign. "Yeah. Can't I come back to the 'Vi-park for a while?"

"Nope." Josh sounds very decided. "What if someone sees you?"

"Good point." He climbs past me to the door, tucking Perky into his large jacket pocket. "Oh, I'm leaving Trudy's dress in here. Is that okay? I don't want to be caught with it. Doesn't prove anything if it's found here."

"Good thinking," I say, giving his shoulder a quick squeeze in lieu of a hug. "I'll be in touch as soon as Dad is officially found, okay?"

"Yep!" Beaming, he climbs down, slams the door, and waves cheerily to us as we pull away.

Well, at least he's happy.

What, and I'm not?

I am, I just…I feel like my insides are in a blender, that's all. So many thoughts keep flying through my head. What if…what if, now Dad knows it wasn't Mau's fault, he blames *me* for Carol's death?

"Shall we grab some take-out?" Father Ben's deep voice snaps my attention back out of my head.

It's mid-afternoon now, and we haven't eaten lunch. Technicolor had stocked the cupboards with non-perishables, which kept us going while we were out-city, but I'm not surprised when Josh nods immediately. "Good plan."

I shrug. I'm sure they're both hungry. Me, I'm not sure I could eat anything.

One bite of delicious noodles, once we're parked in the 'Vi-park—still empty—and I realize how ravenous I am. I dig in with proper enthusiasm. We've almost finished when a small engine draws up beside us.

Josh glances outside—his hand clenches on his carton, crumpling it.

"What is *she* doing here?" he snarls.

I peer out the window and see a small, familiar, much-hated turquoise car. "Fernanda!"

Good thing we did drop Harry off.

There's a rap on the door.

"You think if I roar loudly enough like a rex she'll fall over on her frilly behind?" asks Josh.

Father Ben quickly hides a smile. "I think you'd better open up."

Sighing, Josh hits the open button. I smell the cloying apple perfume before I've even managed to focus on her.

Head-to-toe in turquoise, of course. Smart attire, today, a neat skirt and jacket. Shoes with enough heel to make her look even more out of place here.

"Ah, Mr. Wilson," she chirps, "May I come in?"

"No," says Josh, which is about the rudest thing a hunter—or farmer, come to that—could say in the circumstances, though the full significance is probably lost on her.

"But I'll get a crook in my neck if I have to look up at you like this."

"You'd better make it quick, then," suggests Josh.

Fernanda's lips tighten. She peers up past Josh, her eyes fixing on me, then Father Ben. "It's more Darryl I wanted to see. Are you sure I can't come up?"

"What do you want?" I ask quickly, since Josh is simmering unusually close to the boil, and her asking a second time to come in is at least as rude as him refusing her in the first place.

"Presumably you have abandoned any ambition to gain custody of Harry." Her eyes spark with triumph, at having my duplicity laid bare for all to see. "It came to my attention that you left the city yesterday with Joshua Wilson."

"So? I'm an adult."

"Joshua Wilson, along with the priest who aided and abetted you before, and a teenage hunter girl. Is she in there?"

Josh rolls his eyes. "It ain't unusual for teenage hunters to get lifts with whoever's going the right way. No one else in here now except us."

"You know what I think?" Fernanda's voice is unusually sharp.

"I don't think any of us care what you think," retorts Josh.

I try to elbow in front of him, afraid he's bringing the hostility too far into the open.

Fernanda continues as though he hasn't spoken. "I think that 'girl' was Harry. And if I prove it, not only will you, Darryl, never be gaining custody of Harry, ever, but I will personally ensure that you, Mr. Wilson, and you, Father Benedictine, go back to prison where you unquestionably belong!"

So much for *Josh* bringing the hostilities to the surface! I give up.

"Josh is right," I say flatly. "None of us care."

Father Ben opens his mouth as though considering some diplomatic remark, then sighs and closes it again. Josh is just reaching for the door 'close' button when a police car turns into the 'Vi-park and pauses—reading registration plates?—then heads our way. Josh stiffens, tension radiating from him. I grab his hand and hold it as he makes an instinctive twitch toward the cab. He clutches back, sweat breaking out on his palm.

Fernanda purses her lips in a satisfied way. "Ah, maybe someone is going to beat me to it."

Only a single officer steps from the car, though, and approaches the open door with an easy smile on her middle-aged face. "I'm looking for Darryl Franklyn? City-gate showed her entering with this vehicle a short time ago?"

"Here." My insides unknot. Mostly. It's about Dad, isn't it?

"Could I come in for a moment?"

"Of course," says Josh, relaxing a little, though not all the way.

Is Dad okay?

The officer climbs in easily, clearly in good shape. Despite her shoes, Fernanda manages to ooze right up behind her, like syrup dripping off a countertop but in reverse. In the presence of the cop, Josh doesn't pick her up and pitch her bodily back out again, but he only unfolds a chair for the invited visitor, leaving Fernanda to hover nosily at the cop's elbow, displaying her CPS ID ostentatiously as though it gives her the right to be there.

"Ms. Franklyn, I have some very unexpected news for you," says—Officer MacNamara, reads her badge—smiling in a rather maternal way as she meets my eyes. "It may come as a considerable shock—but a happy one, I'm sure. Your father was left outside the gate of your family farm late this morning—unconscious but alive—by persons unknown, and discovered there by a neighbor, who brought him right away for medical treatment. It turns out he was only tranquilized and has no other injuries, although the hospital wants to keep him overnight for observation and a full police medical examination since it would appear that he was a victim of kidnapping. Uh, just as you and your brother alleged some months ago, I believe."

I try to imagine that I'm hearing this totally unexpectedly. "A-a-alive?" I stutter. "He's really alive?"

"Alive and perfectly well."

"Do you know who—?"

Officer MacNamara grimaces. "Unfortunately, the kidnappers seem to have been very careful. He never saw their faces, or where he was held. He was tranquilized whenever he was being moved anywhere. We have a possible lead as to who was behind it all, but it's far too soon to say whether that will come to anything."

I exchange a smile with Josh and Father Ben. Officer MacNamara will assume we're just happy about Dad being alive—really, we're celebrating the initial success of our plan to keep Mau out of jail.

Fernanda stands rigid, her face frozen. "Alive?" she finally squeaks. "Their father is alive?"

"He is indeed," says Officer MacNamara, scratching the graying hair at her temple. "Always a great day when one gets to deliver this kind of news, wouldn't you agree?"

Josh opens his mouth, his eyes on Fernanda—but then he draws in a deep breath, nostrils flaring, and closes it again. Self-control—and forgiveness?—reasserting itself?

"Of...of course," Fernanda agrees, looking like she's bitten into a lemon. "That poor boy," she whispers to herself.

"What's that?" asks the cop.

"The boy. Only fifteen. They'll take him back out-city." She tuts, shaking her head. "Sad. So very sad. But if the father is alive... Excuse me. It would appear there is nothing more I can do here. There are other cases needing my time." She gropes around for the door button—Josh hits it for her.

She climbs awkwardly down, gets into her car, and drives away, leaving nothing but a sickly cloud of apple scent behind. Hopefully that's the last we'll ever see of *her*!

"Darryl," says Father Ben, "I can give you a lift to the hospital. We can pick up Harry en route."

"Thank you! Oh, which hospital?" I ask Officer MacNamara.

"Exception Central."

A shadow passes over Josh's face, for some reason, then he smiles again, offering suitable thanks and goodbyes as Officer MacNamara also departs. I climb down with Father Ben and get into the SOS van.

Josh follows us and stands by my open door.

"Well, I'll probably see you tomorrow," I say, grinning. No more Fernanda to worry about! "Uh…" I feel my face fall. "If you're hanging around, anyway?" Will he want to drive straight back out into the wilderness again? He shouldn't go alone, but that might not stop him.

But he smiles back, his rich chocolate-brown eyes reflecting the same delight at having Fernanda out of our hair. "I'll stick around until you guys head out-city. So drop in any time."

Father Ben gives Josh a smile and says, "Let's meet tomorrow, before I go out-city again."

"Sure. Message me with a time," says Josh.

I want to ask what that's about, but keep my mouth shut. Maybe it's for confession, or spiritual direction or…or just for a post-prison chat. None of my business.

I wave to Josh as we pull away, but I'm too lost in my own thoughts to talk as we drive through the city traffic. Once again, I'm acutely aware that I should feel happy—and that I do. But only in my head. My body feels—turmoil. Terrible, total turmoil. That queasy feeling is back. I'm on my way to be reunited with Dad. Dad who I've dreamed of finding alive for so long. Dad who we tried so hard, took such risks, sacrificed so much, to try to find. I guess I am real worried about him, though.

Tomorrow, will I be back on the farm, with Dad and Harry? No need to flee anywhere with Josh, now.

Which is a good thing, right? We don't have to risk trouble with the law. No question of Josh going back to prison.

Finding Dad is a good thing.

Harry and I going back to the farm is a good thing.

So why do I just feel like I wanna cry?

JOSHUA

It seems very quiet in the 'Vi when Darryl and Father Ben have gone. I fold the extra chairs and put them away, then take a cup of Jo up the turret and try to relax. Shame I can't leave the city, but I'd have to go alone, and I really don't wanna leave until Darryl and Harry do—especially after saying I'll be here. The next few days could be stressful for them and the 'Vi might provide them with a safe haven where they can just… take a breather. Now Fernanda is finally outta our hair.

Good riddance.

I don't have to risk prison, nor Darryl, neither, by attempting to carry Harry away with us.

That's cause for celebration, right?

I feel terrible tense, though. Like there's a storm coming. I check the weather report on the console, but there ain't no weather warnings. It's just my emotions, I guess. Too much going on.

It's stupid, considering how very much I don't wanna ever go back to jail, but I actually feel real disappointed.

I mean, don't get me wrong, I'm happy for Darryl and Harry, *real* happy. The very thought of how I would feel, if Dad were suddenly alive again…oh yeah, I'm happy for them.

Personally, though, I guess I'd have preferred to be on route to another state, a fresh start with my little family.

Now, it almost feels like they suddenly ain't my family no more. Because they've got their dad back. Their farm. Everything like before. They don't need me. They don't need the 'Vi. This ain't gonna be their home again after all.

And that really hurts.

I know I'm being kinda stupid. The fact that they don't live here no more don't change how we feel about each other, what we've been through together. I'm sure they don't suddenly consider me not-family. I know that.

It's just how it *feels*.

I try to push the thoughts away. What did Harry say that one time? That I should consider their farm my camp? Except it ain't their farm, no more, to offer me. It's their dad's again. Is he gonna like me? Want me around? He obviously needs to heal. And they'll all need to settle in as a family again. I'll have to give them some space.

But I can visit, right? I just mustn't overstay my welcome.

My mind strays back to that wonderful moment when I opened the 'Vi door and Darryl were here. Have I hurt her feelings, though? 'Cause I didn't cry? Did she notice? I'm still in-city, and even if I weren't, I'm not sure I could've. Feels like a valve is stuck or some'at. She didn't act like she noticed. I'm probably worrying for nothing.

I sip my coffee and wish the gnats would stop fluttering around my stomach. I seem to have swallowed a whole swarm. Their dad's alive. This is a very happy day.

Sighing, I drink more Jo, glad of the warmth because evening is approaching, and it's cold tonight, winter gathering momentum.

"Tomorrow, Bear," I murmur, glancing down toward the cupboard below where that urn nestles discreetly, "I'm speaking to Father Ben about how to arrange a proper burial."

Mebbe Darryl and Harry can come along to that. Well, Darryl, anyway. Harry ain't said another word about Wilhelm. Let's hope nothing eats him before he gets done "processing."

My eyes search the sky, inch by inch, scanning the clouds, hunting for storm signs, but there's nothing. Before I realize what I'm doing, I'm checking the weather again. Nothing. The radar around Exception City shows nothing the forecasters have missed, neither.

I'm just tense 'cause since I got outta prison yesterday morning everything I expected to happen in the near future has changed completely, like, three times over. I go back to my coffee.

I've just put my empty mug down when an unfamiliar 'Vi turns into the park and begins maneuvering into position at the far end. I stare at it, assaulted by a niggling sense of familiarity—though I'm sure I ain't seen it before. Has someone described it to me?

Grabbing my binos, I check the registration

number: HUH6 JFK4.

My already gnat-ridden belly chills, all the hairs standing up down my back. I focus on the cab, where I can just make out a slender figure behind the wheel.

Seb.

What in Saint Des's name is he *doing here?*

Don't miss Book 11 – Weigh the Odds

You can make a difference!

Reviews and recommendations are vital to any author's success. If you liked this book, please write a short review—a few lines are enough—and tell your friends about the book too.
You will help the author to create new stories and allow others to share your enjoyment.

Your support is important. Thank you.

*Don't miss the rest of
the unSPARKed series.*

PICK UP BOOKS 1-9 TODAY!

DON'T FORGET THE PREQUELS!

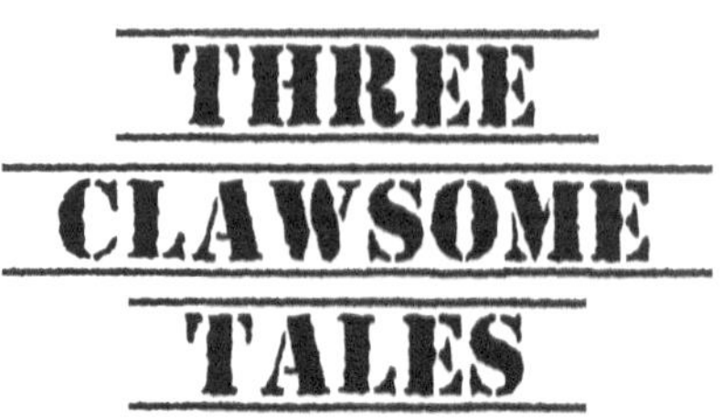

Three unSPARKed short stories now available as a paperback.

LIAM AND THE HUNTERS OF LEE'VI

Can they find his family before it's too late?

It's Christmas week, but sixteen-year-old Tam and the hunters of the Lee'Vi are out looking for a pack of Utahraptors. Instead, they find a boy staggering through the snow, on a mission to save his family. Can they find them before it's too late?

A TRULY CLAWFUL CHRISTMAS

Can he survive Christmas?

If young city-priest Father Benedict can't find more volunteers for his Christmas Bazaar, he'll have to cancel it. But an unexpected appeal from his bishop leaves him facing a very different Christmas. Suddenly, complaints from disappointed parishioners are the least of his worries. His new priority— survival!

A VERY JURASSIC LENT

Perfect faith—like Saint Desmond.

When a risky Ash Wednesday mission to sterilize T. rex eggs goes wrong, fasting is the least of Joshua, Darryl, and Harry's worries. Can they survive a protective Rex Momma and a pack of raptors, or will their Lent begin with tragedy?

All 3 short stories available separately as eBooks.

TURN OVER FOR A SNEAK PEEK

LIAM AND THE HUNTERS OF LEE'VI

"See anything, Tam?"

"Nah. These Utahraptors are ghosts, far as I can tell." I lower my binoculars for a moment, flexing my stiff shoulders.

"They ain't ghosts." Jace continues quartering his quadrant without pause. "Farmers don't pay good money to have ghosts culled. Keep looking. Remember, if we get them before the New Year round-up, there's a bonus."

Sighing, I raise my binos again. I've been zooming in and out for so long my finger is getting tired.

Out of the corner of my eye, I catch the movement as Jace elbows Marty sharply in the ribs. "Marty! Wake up or forfeit your share, you lazy—"

Marty raises his head with a grunt, fumbling with his binos. "Hey, the boy's right, Jace. These critters are keeping a real low profile."

"So we outwait them, thicko."

Marty sighs even louder than I did and claps the binos to his eyes. From what I've seen so far, he's the easiest going of the three. And Jace is the boss—owns a full half of the habitat vehicle whereas Marty and Roddy only own a quarter each—so he can be freer with the name-calling than the rest of us. A hundred times freer than me, who don't own nothing. I'm just the assistant. Still, I ain't complaining. I could be back with—

Movement… I spin the wheel of the binos quickly, tensing. Then sigh again. "Just deinons." The pair of tan and cream deinonychuses, standing barely as high as a short man, ain't what we're after.

"Should we try a new spot?" says Roddy.

"Let's give it a few more hours here." Jace carries on scanning as he speaks. "We're smack in the heart of their territory and we've been here long enough they'll be losing their caution even if they did notice us arrive. We move and we risk scaring them off and having to wait all over again."

"Do raptors scare off that easily?" I ask.

An ominous silence from Jace…

"That were a serious question!" I say quickly. "Do they?"

"Not if they can see tasty little people walking around, sure, no." Jace has decided to give me the benefit of the doubt. "But a large, strange-smelling vehicle? They're smart enough to be wary."

"And we want them all in our sights before we fire, remember," says Roddy. "Or we'll be chasing all over after the stragglers."

"I know *that*," I say indignantly.

"All right, city-born. Keep your wig on."

That only makes me throw him a glare. I can't help being city-born. Some hunters are way too proud of the fact that their grandparents didn't flee to the cities like most people did after the government declared the escaped 're-creations' uncontainable. He just ignores me, though. At sixteen, I'm very much the cub in this den.

I return my attention to my section of wilderness, out there beyond the turret windows. Snow blankets the ground. "At least they'll be easy to spot," I point out. Their grey feathers should show up well against the white, their colored ruffs even more so.

"If they ever show themselves at all," grumbles Marty, but he's diligently checking his quadrant now. Doesn't want to miss his share, especially not when there's a bonus in the offing. I'm excited about the bonus, too. As a mere assistant, I get a fixed wage instead of a percentage share—and bonus money for me is up to Jace. But he says it's Christmas week and I'm out here working the same as them, so this time, I'll get a fifth share. *If* we can catch the Utahraptors before the hill farmers head out to round up their wild-roaming stock in three days time.

I begin a new sweep—then swing the binos quickly as another movement catches my eye. Probably that pair of deinons again…yep, there they are, high-stepping eagerly through the snow, heads stretched out. Following some tempting scent. I scan ahead of them, looking for something moving…

There. What the—?

"Boy! There's a *boy!*"

"A *what?*"

"A boy! Three o'clock, six hundred feet, *look!*"

I dump the binos on the console ledge, fumbling for my rifle. By the time I've got it aimed, Marty's raised the windows and Jace is on our side of the turret, his own rifle pointing the right way, though he immediately drops one hand to the Intercar button, flipping the loudspeaker switch.

The boy, slender and dark haired, is staggering through the snow as though he can barely walk, oblivious to the danger closing in from behind. As Jace's voice booms from the Habitat Vehicle's external speakers he stumbles, his head jerking up.

"Run, kid! There's a pair of carni'saurs on your tail!"

The boy stares around, his eyes darting over his shoulder, looking for the danger, then wildly scanning in our direction as he tries to spot us. With the hab'vi well muffled in camo netting and a layer of snow, it's no surprise we're invisible. I mean, that's the idea.

Jace's hand moves, swiping on the strobe light on top of the turret, sending eerie flickers dancing over the white landscape.

"Here! We've got you covered, but shift yourself!"

The boy lurches forward at a faster pace, but it's clear even the news about the two hungry carni'saurs isn't enough to get him running. But the deinons have slowed to a halt, peering towards the 'Vi. Or rather, the eye-searing light. Guess they don't know what it is and they're not sure they want to find out. With four crosshairs on them, they got that right.

"Get below and help him in, Tam," orders Jace. "He looks beat."

"Sure thing." I slide down the ladder into the Vi's main living area and move to the side door, pushing the button to make it slide back. Leaving my rifle just inside the door where I can grab it if I really need to, I drop down into the snow and go the last few steps to meet the boy. He's younger than me—several years younger. What the heck is he doing out here?

"Come on, it's okay." Catching his arm, I help him to the 'Vi and boost him up into it. With the huge ground clearance of a Hab'Vi, the floor level is higher than his head. Rolling up and in after him—I'm still a little too short for leaping in to be that easy—I hit the door close button and call up to the turret, "Clear."

The boy's lying on the floor, panting and shivering—cold or exertion or both. "Hey, you okay?" I help him sit up. "You're safe now. Relax."

"My family." His accent's strange, and he gasps the words, still panting hard. "We've got to get to my family!"

"Are they out there too?" My heart sinks.

The boy nods, flopping against the wall as though he can barely sit upright.

Jace's booted feet touch the floor with a soft thud. Roddy's already sliding down after him.

"His family are out there," I say urgently.

Jace swears, crouching beside the boy. "Hey, kid, whereabouts are your family? How far away?"

"I..." The boy struggles to keep his head up, his face drawn with exhaustion. "I've been walking since...since early this morning."

Early this morning? Aw, heck! It's two in the afternoon now.

Jace's face tightens into grim lines and Roddy winces. Jace scoops the kid up with a grunt of exertion—the boy ain't *that* young—and deposits him in the chair in front of the console. Swiping quickly at the screen, Jace brings up a map of the area, demanding, "Are they in a vehicle or on foot? Do you know where?"

"Vehicle," whispers the weary boy. "We were...we were driving along the minor road... the snow slipped... swept us off the road, down a hillside. My parents were unconscious..." He leans forward, his eyes frantically searching the map, dazed with fatigue, "my sisters, they were okay, but Abby had banged her knee... So...I came alone to find help...trying to cut across...reach the main highway..."

"Never mind that now." Jace's voice is soft. Soothing. "Just concentrate on the map. Where are they?"

The boy puts a hand on either side of the screen, staring down at it. Finally, after what seems like forever, his gaze firms and his finger moves to point at a small road ten miles to the north. "There. That was the road."

"Certain?"

"Yeah. I was reading the map for Dad. We were on that road when the avalanche happened."

"Okay." Jace turns his head to say, "Roddy, get us moving. Marty, back up the turret and keep a look-out. We need to move fast. Tam, get some hot food and drink for…what's your name, kid?"

The boy's head is drooping towards his chest, but he raises it again. "Liam. Liam McEvoy."

"Get some food for Liam. My name's Jace, Jace Lee, and this is the Lee'Vi. That's Marty gone up the turret and Roddy in the cab, my co-owners, and this cub's Tam, our assistant."

I'm not sure if Liam hears the introductions. "Will we be in time?" On his face, dread wars with painful hope.

"We'll get there as fast as we can, and you got here as fast as you could, clear enough, so there ain't nothing more that can be done."

Small comfort, if it ain't enough, but what can he say?

"Tam, soon as Liam's had something to eat and drink, get him in a sleeping bag to warm up and catch some Zs." He jabs a finger over his shoulder.

"What?" Liam struggles to sit up straight. "No, I can't sleep. My family—"

"When we reach the road, we're gonna need you rested and alert so you can tell us where it happened. We don't wanna drive right past. So for your family's sake, you need to rest while you can. Understood?"

Liam nods uncertainly. Jace probably seems alarmingly rough-spoken and abrupt. I remember when I first went to live with Uncle Mike, I thought he was angry every time he said anything, until I learned that hunters just don't mince their words the way city-folk do.

I start to make oatmeal on the stovetop, staggering now and then as the vehicle lurches and slides through the snow. Oatmeal's filling and quick. Jace makes a hot drink straight from the boiler tap, presses it into Liam's hands, and heads up the turret to join Marty. Coffee, but there's no chance it's going to keep Liam awake, in his condition. Soon I'm swapping the empty mug for a bowl of oatmeal.

"Here you go. Get that inside you."

Liam tucks in, his spoon moving in a rather stop-start manner as tiredness fights with hunger. But he soon pauses to look at me.

"Will we be in time?"

Aw, heck. "I, uh, I dunno. What sort of car was it? A city-car?" Not that raptors couldn't have peeled the stronger grilles off even a farm truck ten times over, by now. Grilles only provide good protection for a moving vehicle. And there's a pack of huge Utahraptors around here somewhere. Even bigger than a Dakotaraptor, taller than a tall man and many times longer. Unaccounted for.

Oh God, no. My stomach lurches. Is our missing quarry off devouring this boy's family? Is that why they haven't shown themselves around here? No, a Utahraptor pack's territory is huge, no reason it should be that.

Liam's nodding seriously in answer to my question. "We don't usually drive out-city much. We're on our way to spend New Year's Eve with our Uncle Greg. He moved to Exception State to take up an opportunity training thoroughbred dracorex for the racetrack there."

"Where are you coming from?" His accent ain't from around here, that's for sure.

"Kitchener, Ontario."

"Ontario? Where's that?"

He looks surprised. "Canada."

"Canada? Oh." That's like, a different *country*, right? "I dunno if I've ever met anyone from Canada."

"You have now. But it *was* a city-car. So, will we be in time?"

I spread my hands helplessly. "It's not really something I can predict. I mean, city-folk assume if you step foot outside your vehicle you'll be eaten on the spot, but that ain't true. I mean, if you pulled up somewhere quietly, especially in a 'Vi, without doing anything to attract attention, and you kept alert, you could take a walk and nine times out of ten, maybe even ninety-nine times out of a hundred, you'd get away with it. But the tenth—or hundredth—time you'd get eaten. And you get to ten—or even a hundred—very quick if you do it a lot, which is why hunters never ever go out-vehicle without cover.

"But, uh," reluctantly, I continue, "it's a fact that a broken down vehicle's more at risk. Even if a carni'saur doesn't know there may be people in it, it's still gonna attract attention. So if I said anything other than that *I don't know*, I'd be lying."

Get
THREE CLAWSOME TALES
as a paperback today!

Or pick up
'Liam and the Hunters of Lee'Vi'
from your favorite ebook retailer.

ABOUT THE AUTHOR

Corinna Turner has been writing since she was fourteen and likes strong protagonists with plenty of integrity. Although she spends as much time as possible writing, she cannot keep up with the flow of ideas, for which she offers thanks—and occasional grumbles!—to the Holy Spirit. She is the author of over twenty-five books, including the Carnegie Medal Nominated I Am Margaret series, and her work has been translated into four languages. She was awarded the St. Katherine Drexel award in 2022.

She is a Lay Dominican with an MA in English from Oxford University and lives in the UK. She is a member of a number of organizations, including the Society of Authors, the Catholic Writers Guild, Catholic Teen Books, Catholic Reads, the Angelic Warfare Confraternity, and the Sodality of the Blessed Sacrament. She used to have a Giant African Land Snail, Peter, with a 6½" long shell, but now makes do with a cactus and a campervan.

Get in touch with Corinna...

Facebook: Corinna Turner

Twitter: @CorinnaTAuthor

www.ingramcontent.com/pod-product-compliance
Lightning Source LLC
Chambersburg PA
CBHW031250210726
48287CB00003B/969